HIGHLAND SLIGHT

OF JUSTICE

COLIN MCPHAIL

First published in Great Britain in 2006 by Ocean Wheels
Merlin House, 5, Crossway, Hillend Industrial Park,
Dalgety Bay, Fife, KY11 9JE

Copyright © 2005 Colin McPhail MBE
Cover illustration copyright © Robert McPhail
Cover illustration from original artwork by Robert McPhail

A CIP catalogue record for this book is available from the British Library

ISBN 0 9551519 0 2
ISBN 978 0 9551519 0 3

Printed and bound in Great Britain by Antony Rowe Ltd

*This novel is dedicated to my wife Corrie for her love,
care and devotion during my recent illness.*

Best Wishes
Colin McPhail

AUTHOR BIOGRAPHY – COLIN MCPHAIL

From Scottish and Welsh descent, Colin McPhail was born in London during the war in May 1940 and temporarily evacuated to Suffolk with his family as the bombing of the city worsened. After the war back in London, he was brought up with a Dutch stepfather and received a Grammar School education to become a chartered civil engineer taking up various posts in local government. In 1995, he chaired a working group whilst employed by Lothian Regional Council to produce the "Edinburgh Streetscape Manual" and has since written appendices to the manual. In 1996 after 36 year's in local government he took early retirement but carried on working as a private consultant.

He has been a community councillor for 24 years on Dalgety Bay and Hillend Community Council in Fife and been its Chairman for the past 18 years seeing the growth of the new town of Dalgety Bay to a population of around 12000.

He has also served 10 years in the volunteer Royal Naval Auxiliary Service (RNXS) ending up as its Head of Unit at Rosyth on the disbandment of the service in 1994 following the end of the Cold War. Since then, he has served a period as Chairman of the local Sea Cadets and up until last year been a member of the Maritime Volunteer Service's National Council.

In 2004, he was awarded the MBE in the Queen's Birthday Honours List for services to the community of Dalgety Bay. He is married to a Dutch wife with three sons and apart fom writing this book, which is his first novel, his other interests are football, art and amateur dramatics playing various roles on stage in pantomimes, plays and musicals.

HIGHLAND SPIRIT OF JUSTICE

Contents

Chapter 1 – Tragedy

Chapter 2 – Escape

Chapter 3 – Journey to the New World

Chapter 4 – The New World

Chapter 5 - New World Descendants

Chapter 6 – Glen Beag Visit

Chapter 7 – Spirits of the Glen

Appendix of terms

HIGHLAND SPIRIT OF JUSTICE

Chapter 1 – Tragedy

The Highland Clearances were in full swing; Calum Mcdonall in Glean Bheag never considered evictions would affect him and his family who etched out a living from a croft in a more remote part of the glen. The croft was a new construction for the Highlands as he had rebuilt it in dry stone walling and rendered it with mortar with a thatched roof covering a timber frame . It was also different to other crofts, because as part of the reconstruction, Calum had incorporated chimney flues at each gable end. The glen belonged to Mcdonall of Glean Bheag who relied on some two hundred clansmen with their families living in the glen to pay him rent.

His loyalty to his Clan Chief was never in question and following the 1745 rebellion, his family continued to scratch out an existence in the poor soil with the usual crop of oats, some barley and potatoes. He also had a number of chickens, sheep, geese and a few head of milking cows. As a supplement whenever possible, he fished in the nearby loch and hunted wild game to provide fresh meat for his family.

It was now September 1780, a good thirty-five years since his late father was called out and involved in the ill-fated Jacobite rebellion. Some twelve years ago his parents died from distemper and were buried in the clan burial place at the mouth of the glen. He was thirty-six years old, of medium build and height with dark hair and a ruddy complexion. He had a wife Siobhan who was of a vivacious nature and delicately built with pretty brown eyes on an attractive well-featured face. She had flowing black hair that came down from her head to her shoulders. He loved her deeply along with his young sons Calum and Cailean aged eight and five who were becoming more rugged and adventurous each day.

He'd lived all of his life on the croft being brought up proud and resourceful in true highland tradition, never being afraid of hard work. As an early teenager, it was at one of the annual gatherings when he first met Siobhan who was four years his junior and this led them to start meeting at a secret place in the glen and playing together. From this innocent enjoyment of playing together, their relationship blossomed as they grew up from friendship into affection and deep love for each other.

She was the daughter of Ranald and Elspeth Mcdonall who were the gardner and head maid at Ardonall House, the clan chief's residence and as she grew up she befriended the chief's youngest daughter who taught her to read and write.

She was given a pleasant upbringing at the "Big Hoose" as she nicknamed it and was well treated by the chief's family.

The only flaw in her time living there was the continual pestering she received from the young randy Murdo Mcdonnall who was the hereditary chief tacksman to the clan chief and lived in a house of favour on the estate. He was nine years older than Siobhan and was ruthless in carrying out his chief's instructions.

He was of medium height, plump and muscular with a square shaped head that had a face cratered from acne. He continually smelt of body odour and reeked bad breadth. She couldn't bear the sight of him and as she grew up she tried to avoid him as much as possible.

However, his pestering turned into sexual intent and things came to a head as she turned sixteen when one evening after earlier fending off his advances during an unaccompanied walk in the house gardens, he leapt out at her from behind a tall privet hedge and forced her to the ground. He then frenziedly started to tear off her clothes. She screamed and fought, scratching him in his face but his huge weight overpowered her as she desperately struggled to fend him off. He was down to feverishly undoing the laces on her bodice with his sweaty hands when he was interrupted by;

"Murdo, what's going on there?"

He recognised the chief's voice shouting from his study where he'd been interrupted by the noise.

"Oh its alright, I'm just freeing Siobhan from the brambles" Murdo replied. Then looking at the anguish on Siobhan's face he told her,

"You keep your mouth shut about this do yer ken? Otherwise yer mother and father will be oot of work".

"I want you to come to the study and help me with these papers" called the chief.

"Aye, I'm coming Sir" he answered as he reluctantly loosened his grip on Siobhan allowing her to get up. He then headed off towards the house..

Siobhan in a state of shock rose to her feet, quickly gathered up her clothes and ran to the servant's quarters. She felt abused and dirty and after washing herself down, changed into a clean dress. When her mother asked her about the torn one she kept to the story that it had been torn on the brambles. The following day, to cover up, Murdo instructed her father to trim back the brambles on the estate.

After this incident with Murdo, she made up her mind to leave Ardonall House at the earliest opportunity. When she next met Calum she purposely didn't tell him about Murdo's attack in order to protect her parent's jobs. She avoided Murdo over the next few weeks until she was again confronted by him in the grounds when he grabbed her and said; "Be here tomorrow evening after supper, I want to finish what I started". She trembled as he looked at her with lust in his eyes. She knew she must be free of his advances and that evening told her parents she was leaving to live with Calum. Without knowing the real reason for her departure, they tried at first to dissuade her but once they knew her mind had been made up, they agreed with the knowledge that when she was with Calum she was happy and contented and of course, that she would still be living in the same glen

Early next morning she gathered her belongings together, kissed her parents goodbye and without being seen, headed off up the glen to meet Calum. She felt as though a heavy burden had been lifted as she freely skipped along the track that took her up to the upper part of the glen to meet the one she loved. He gave her a long and lingering kiss that took her breath away after she told him she wanted to be with him as his wife. He was not sure of what his parents would say, but when he brought her home they were very pleased that they were going to marry and make their home there. With the blessing of both sets of parents, Siobhan persuaded him to journey to Inverness and marry. In her mind this would avoid her facing Murdo who would have been invited if the wedding were to be held in the glen. As it turned out, he was furious when he heard they'd married.

For the next four years they lived with his parents in the family croft until they died from distemper, which ravaged the glen decimating the elderly population. On the death of his parents, Calum rebuilt the croft to make it a good home for Siobhan and their bairns who were born in 1772 and 1775; both after his parents died. She dearly loved him and their bairns, feeling safe and protected living in the croft.

Her mother and father continued to work at the "Big Hoose" and visited them and their bairns until one day, Murdo suddenly sacked them on his chief's instruction. This was due to the estate's mounting debts. Luckily for them, they were offered similar employment at another mansion house in England but this prevented them from travelling back to Scotland and seeing the family in Glean Bheag.

This time of the year in September, the morning mists hung heavily above the glen's loch and was only penetrated by the tall trees on its island showing through its eerie wisps. The dew also lay thick in the heather that was now well in bloom. The only sound was the occasional calls of capercallies and grouse on the muir accompanied by the snorting of deer as they drank with slurps at the loch side. For Calum, life continued at its normal pace as he was making room for the storage of the croft's meagre crop and turf from his peat dig, ready to meet the oncoming winter. Glean Bheag was narrow and u-shaped at its top end, having an atmospheric beauty of its own this time of year from the purple colour of its heathery slopes interrupted with green patches of gorse and the occasional hazel scrub.

Then one morning later in the month a tacksman who he knew as Hector arrived to deliver a letter written in English. He could not contain himself to know what was in it and being not able to read or write, he asked Hector to read it to him.

"I'm afraid its bad news, it's a notice which requires you and your family to leave the croft within the next thirty days or be forcibly evicted and I'm instructed to hand this notice over to you by order of the Chief Tacksman Murdo Mcdonall."

Siobhan shuddered on the mention of his name. Murdo had signed it on behalf of the chief and no reason was given as to why they had to leave their croft. Calum was outraged and asked Siobhan who was more learned than him to write back declaring his family's loyalty to the clan chief and his plight of having to support a wife and two young bairns. He also volunteered to pay the chief higher dues for the occupation of the land that had been inhabited by generations of his family over the past two hundred and thirty years. The reply, written inside the croft by a frightened Siobhan on a sheet of parchment using her quill pen was signed with his mark and duly given to Hector for delivery to the chief.

Unbeknown to them, Murdo was looking down at them from a concealed position on the brae above the croft to see what their reaction would be to the notice.

Hector placed the letter in his tunic and climbed back up the hill to where Murdo was concealed.

"Well what did they say?" Murdo asked as Hector joined him.

"They've written a letter to the chief protesting against the eviction notice" he answered.

"Ooch let me see it". Hector handed over the letter; Murdo glanced at it before placing it in his pocket.

"Aye as I thought, its been written by Siobhan, I've unfinished business with that fine lass; Do yer ken! I'm longing to bed her if I can get rid of Calum. Aye I must have her" Murdo lustily remarked.

They both then made their way to Murdo's house exchanging rude jokes about Siobhan and talked of what they would like to do to her. Weeks passed and as there was no further correspondence or visits to the croft by the tacksman or his men; Calum considered the matter closed. He did not even take the bother to seek an audience with the clan chief. In his mind, he felt the reply had been accepted and went about his daily routine.

It was now the beginning of December and the winter snows had turned the high peaks white on each side of the glen and made them glisten in the winter sun. Rumours had spread that families in the lower part of the glen were being evicted from their homes but he refused to believe it could ever happen to him and his family. After all, he had sent a personal letter to the chief on the matter.

What he had failed to realise was the letter never reached the chief and that the old clan system had been systematically broken after the battle of Culloden in 1746 following the final defeat of the Jacobite cause and clansmen were now being replaced with extensive sheep farming in the glens. There was more money to be made by removing highland families from the glens and replacing them with sheep and creating hunting estates for the lairds. This was far more profitable for the chiefs and their tacksmen. Clan loyalty had been removed by money raising ventures. The depopulation of the highlands had begun which started the decline of highland culture and its language from which it would never recover.

December 6 was the day the whole world fell in upon Calum Mcdonall with a tragic blow that changed his life forever.

The day started well enough, it was dry and crisp following an overnight frost as he kissed his wife and bairns farewell before climbing up towards the corrie slopes to look for missing hens that may have nested there.

His family was his pride and joy having shown them off at the annual gathering held earlier in the year. What he did not know that morning it was the last time he would ever see them.

He searched and searched for the hens only finding one nest with three eggs in it, but on the upper slopes he did find one of his sheep that had been missing since the autumn.

It was late in the afternoon as he descended back down the brae only to round an outcrop to view the smouldering remains of his croft. His first thought was for the safety of his wife and children. He dropped the eggs as panic stricken he leapt over the rocky outcrops and rivulets of wet peat on his descent. On reaching the croft, he shrieked with horror at the smell of burning flesh and the sight of the charred remains of his family inside. He could see from what was left of their corpses that they had knife and sword wounds. His wife had been raped and her throat cut.

The pungent smoke from burning timber overcame him as he pulled their bodies clear of what was once his croft.

He instantly vomited after looking at them then quickly covered over their charred bodies and sat beside them in shock. For the rest of the day he sobbed and howled beside them in disbelief, which went on into the cold night and the following morning.

He came to his senses as daylight broke shaking from the cold. He then carefully wrapped the bodies in any unburnt cloth he could find and carried his wife and two sons to a soft peat bog close to the croft where he buried them marking their burial places with stone cairns. He was not a religious man so he ceremoniously spoke over their graves in gaelic which translated;

" Here lies my family innocent in death as they were during their short life, I return them to the earth to make it richer; let not the clouds of time pass without bringing to justice those who were responsible for their murder".

He was by nature a non-violent man, different from his father who fought with the Jacobites, but the murder of his wife and children and the loss of his home now changed his life and character forever. He felt an inner rage within himself that suddenly boiled to the surface and drove him to scream and shout abuse that echoed down the glen. He knew he must act and seek retribution for the murders.

After composing himself, he went to a hidden crevice on the braes of the mountain where since the rebellion, was hidden his father's broadsword, pistol, targe, dirk, belt and plaid. These were kept dry within the crevice by being neatly wrapped in a thick cloth. He changed his clothes keeping on his shirt and put on the plaid and the rest of the attire arming himself with the weapons, knowing full well the bearing of arms and the wearing of the tartan was banned by an Act of Parliament since 1748. He then set off down the glen, his anger fired by the good memories of the good life he had enjoyed with his family as he passed their favourite spot where the best view could be had of the whole glen. He was going to confront Murdo and if necessary, the clan chief to seek justice and retribution. As he was bearing arms, he crisscrossed his way down and crouched behind boulders from to time carrying out a reconnaissance to avoid detection.

It was dark and late in the evening with a bitterly cold wind blowing from the east. The sky was overcast when he reached Murdo's house. He recovered his breath and took heed of the situation by sheltering in the byre adjacent to the house. Suddenly, he noticed three milking cows. He looked closer and by their familiar markings he realised that they were his. This on top of what had happened enraged him so much he ran from the byre and pounded on the front door of the house where there were sounds of merrymaking coming from within and shouted,

"Come on out you murderer its Calum Mcdonall here!" There was a pause and shuffling of feet that made him feel uneasy. The door opened gradually with tobacco smoke drifting out into the cold air; there was another pause as if time stood still; then a shot was fired which grazed his arm. He could see within the dim light that there were six men inside, Murdo Mcdonall with Hector that delivered the notice; and four of Murdo's henchmen.

He quickly discharged his pistol into a target illuminated in what there was of the light and there was a cry of agony. He thrust his sword at a shadowy figure who cried out in pain. At the same time using his targe he fended off dirk and sword thrusts as he was attacked. He fought a furious sword fight using the skills he'd learnt from his father. Suddenly, he saw the callous face of Murdo who was cocking and aiming a pistol at him.

He slammed the door shut as he discharged it and luckily for him the door was plated with iron and it rebounded inside. There were cries from within as his attackers were hit by the rebound of shot. Momentarily, he caught a glimpse of more men coming towards him from behind the house.

He decided in an instant to retreat into the dark of the night hastily climbing a steep track. He was breathless at times as he stumbled over the rocky outcrops in the darkness but however painful, he dared not make a sound which would have given away his position to Murdo and his men.

He climbed his way up without leaving any tracks, as he knew the terrain like the back of his hand. Behind him there was a continuous noise from random shots being fired; only a few men ventured to pursue him but luckily, in the wrong direction. He climbed up to the high slopes of Bein Bhreac and found a hiding place that afforded him some protection from the weather. It was just below the snow line and made a good resting place for the night. He formed his plaid into a bed and blanket. He felt cold and shivery after the day's events and only fell asleep from exhaustion after turning over in his mind again and again the shock of what had happened to him and his family. He woke up intermittently and quietly sobbed in the blackness of the night thinking about Siobhan and the bairns.

Chapter 2 – Escape

He was woken by the first strands of light reflecting on the snows of Bein Bhreac. His first reaction, once he drank some icy water, washed his face and bathed his wounded arm using water from a nearby burn, was to head back down the mountainside and renew the fight. As there was an overnight frost, he had to tread carefully as he made his way down to a concealed look out point on the brae above Murdo's house. There appeared to be no movement taking place at the house so he waited shivering in the cold wind. Two hours passed by which seemed timeless to him as his limbs became numb with the cold, then the house door opened and four men came out carrying weapons. He charged his pistol as he reckoned he could take these on, but stopped short when he caught a glimpse of what he thought was about forty Redcoat soldiers coming down the glen to join them. It was obvious they were going to join Murdo and his men to hunt him.

It seemed pointless putting up a fight against these odds; to him digression seemed the better part of valour, so he decided to seek out information and help from someone he could trust in the only settlement in the glen. He climbed back up the mountain making sure those gathering below did not observe him. He then cut across the slope taking a track to the settlement that was only known to a few people.

By midday, he was entering the settlement. He was very cautious: the inhabitants looked sullen and downtrodden. He went to Alastair the glen's smithy that was his childhood friend. Alastair was the same age as him and about the same height being well built for a blacksmith. He had a handsome and jovial face with long fair hair that flowed down to meet his sturdy shoulders. As you would expect, for a blacksmith, his biceps on his arms were huge but not out of character for his athletic body. As boys they regularly went out together to hunt for deer and grouse in the glen.

"Why is everybody so unhappy?" he asked.

"We have just been issued a thirty day notice to quit the glen and we've just heard that your croft was burnt doon yesterday with you family inside; it was a terrible deed and unforgivable" replied Alastair.

At that instant the Redcoat soldiers with Murdo and his men arrived in the settlement. Had they picked up his tracks?

"They are hunting me after I attacked Murdo's house last night" he said "Hide in my hay loft" said Alastair "I'll find out what is happening".

Alastair approached Murdo and his men, as the soldiers surrounded the people of the settlement. There was a crowd muster of some hundred and sixty people. The women and children looked frightened of the Redcoat soldiers. Murdo repeated his thirty-day notice for everyone to quit their homes and said they should not consider pleading with the chief by requesting an audience with him or by writing to him in person. He said the chief was in London over the next few months on business and he, as his chief tacksman, would personally intercept letters. As an example, he produced the letter written by Calum's wife, tore it up infront of them and threw the pieces on the ground.

He warned the inhabitants that harbouring criminals was punishable by death. He asked for any information on Calum who he said attacked his house last night killing his other tacksman and one of his men. He added that there was a reward of £500 for his capture dead or alive. A fair haired soldier who stood out from the others, introduced himself as Captain Baker and told them they would hunt him down like an animal. After Captain Baker had finished speaking there descended an earie silence on the crowd then one of the clansmen stepped forward and indicated that he had seen Calum only that morning heading off in the direction of his croft.

Murdo was dubious with this information and ordered a search of the houses to be quite sure he was being told the truth.

Alastair became uneasy; he was prepared to fight to the death if Calum was discovered and he knew other clansmen would rally round after learning of Calum's plight.

Systematically each house and their outbuildings were searched. When it came to Alastair's hayloft he gritted his teeth as two soldiers went inside. Prodding the hay with their bayonets he waited to hear Calum cry out. There was silence and the soldiers emerged looking satisfied.

Once they had finished their search, Murdo told the inhabitants to send a message to him if they saw Calum. He then departed with his men and the soldiers in the direction given.

Alastair waited until they were well distant before entering the hayloft. "That was a near thing the bayonet only missed me by a hair's breadth" said Calum.

He had also overheard the threats made by Murdo and that he was a wanted man with a price on his head. Once he was outside the hayloft he meticously retrieved the pieces of the torn up letter that had been thrown on the ground by Murdo. As he suspected, it was the letter written by his wife to the clan chief.

He placed the pieces inside his sporran with watery eyes.

"What now?" asked Alastair.

Calum looked at him and the inhabitants with sadness..

"Its no use to keep on fighting them for they will always outnumber us, its just a matter of time before I am caught". He then spoke sternly.

"They may take our homes and livelihood from us and in my case my family, but they cannot touch our spirit which will remain in these glens forever. By removing us they will become responsible for the decline in our way of life and culture and at their barren death their life force will be extinguished with no relief or comfort being given to them for creating a stench of evil throughout their wretched life and bringing misery to this glen".

"I agree with you" said Alastair. "Let the two of us escape and make fresh start in the new world". Calum turned away to wipe his tears.

"Aye" he replied in agreement.

As he had not eaten for the past twenty-four hours, Alastair gave him some oatcakes and whisky, which he consumed hastily; he then packed some food in a bag and attached it to his belt ready for their journey.

As a diversion, to attract the soldiers with Murdo and his men back to the settlement, Alastair set fire to his house and workshop. It quickly raged emitting black smoke that billowed down the glen in their departed direction. Then after bidding farewell to the settlement's residents, they quickly made their way up the brae travelling the opposite way to return to his croft.

They had travelled some two miles when they came upon three of the tacksman's men with a horse and cart containing the sheep, geese and chickens from his croft. They immediately sprang upon them and pulled them off the cart before they could use their weapons. They then bound them up hand and foot.

"Did you get pleasure from seeing my wife and bairns die in the croft you burnt down yesterday?" he asked in an enraged voice.

One of them answered that they were only obeying the instructions of Murdo Mcdonall. He explained that yesterday morning they'd waited for Calum to disappear up into the corrie slopes before approaching his croft. Murdo then tricked Siobhan to open the door and let him inside. They heard screams then silence after waiting outside for twenty minutes. Then Murdo emerged with scratches and blood on his face telling them to burn the croft down. They asked him what had happened to your wife and bairns when he told them to be silent but if anybody asks, to tell them he had accidentally killed them in a fight. He then gulped and continued nervously,

"He then threatened us with our lives if we said otherwise. As I torched your croft I happened to glance through the window and saw your wife lying on the bed raped with her throat cut. Your two bairns were lying dead on the floor with sword and stab wounds. The eldest boy had obviously tried to protect his mother and brother, for he still had a knife in his hand after being run through with Murdo's sword".

They trembled and pleaded for their lives telling Calum that they'd nothing to do with his family's killing only the burning of his croft. Calum continued his rage and shouted at them;

"I am not a religious man by nature, but for revenge, I really ought kill you for what you have done to my family. Instead, I place a curse on you that your evil lives will, by natural causes, soon come to an untimely end".

"Tell Murdo I also place this curse on him, but it be more powerful as it will be passed down through future generations of his family. I also wish the chief of our clan a misfortune for allowing all this to happen to his people".

They untied their prisoner's feet and told them to walk back to the settlement keeping their hands tied behind and not to look back. Frightened and shocked with relief that they were not going to be killed, they stumbled along the track as they slowly made their way down to the black smoke ensuing from the settlement.

They then alighted the cart and drove it back to the remains of his croft where they set the stock free once more. He placed a sprig of heather on his wife and bairns's graves and momentarily paused over them with his own private thoughts.

"We had better get going before they catch up with us" said Alastair. "Unhitch the horse and let it go free as it will make tracks in the wet muir for them to follow".

"I've one thing left to do" said Calum whereon he made his way to the secret crevice in the hillside and changed back into his working clothes wrapping his father's plaid, belt, targe, and broadsword up in the thick cloth and placed them back inside. He held on to his pistol and dirk in case he needed it.

Slapping the horse on its hind quarters they waited momentarily to see it canter off across the muir, then they climbed up to the snow line where there was a mountain track that took them over a pass out of the glen. They stopped and took a last look back knowing full well that this was probably the last time they would ever set eyes on the beautiful glen of Glean Bheag.

They made their way to Fort William avoiding settlements where soldiers were billeted and keeping off the well-trodden tracks.

They passed through one glen that had been cleared of people with its crofts emptied. The winter mists hung heavy in that glen as if it portrayed an air of lament for the departed inhabitants.

It took them a wearisome two days sleeping one night out in the open before they entered Fort William on a cloudy afternoon. The settlement was full of Redcoat soldiers as they made their way down to the harbour where they'd heard that a ship was bound for the Americas.

What they saw was a sorry sight of families that had been evicted from their homes being herded like cattle at gunpoint onto the ship. They kept their emotions under control and their weapons concealed within their clothing.

They found out the ship would be sailing early that evening; by that time most of its passengers would be on board. This amounted to a few hours away and by asking around they were told it was usual for one sentry to be left guarding the boarding gangway.

Calum had no money but Alastair said he had enough for both of their passages. They waited in the shadows and as it was December, it was soon dark by mid-afternoon. As pretence, they approached the sentry singing and making merry holding a flask of whisky inviting him to take a drink. He gratefully took a swig and they quickly nudged past him climbing the gangway calling out for the Captain.

"We would like to join the ship and have good whisky to share with you" shouted Alastair.

The Captain shouted back from his cabin,

"OK you can come aboard but it better be good whisky".

A member of the crew directed them to his cabin where they knocked on the door. He opened it and invited them inside.

"Try it yourself" said Alastair as he placed the flask on the table. The Captain produced three glasses and filled them with the whisky. As they sipped the nectar the Captain smacked his lips with satisfaction.

"We wonder if you have any room onboard for another two passengers?" asked Alastair.

"I say this whisky tastes good, what were you saying? Oh that depends on what you are prepared to pay; sorry let me introduce myself my name is Captain Hocking".

As he introduced himself, Calum noticed he commanded the appearance of a stalwart figure in his tight waistcoat that was worn over a loose flannel shirt tucked into his tight breeches. His brass buttoned, three quarter length blue tunic hung loosely over the chair behind him. He looked between forty and fifty with a well-weathered face and when he spoke it was in a low tone that oozed authority and experience.

Alastair told him what money he had and if it were not enough, that they were prepared to be part of the crew and work their passage. He looked them up and down.

"Agreed" he replied.

He knew full well they could be fugitives from justice however; as he was short of crewmembers for an arduous voyage during winter he decided to take them on.

"Which of the New Colonies are you bound for? asked Alastair.

"Halifax, New Scotia don't worry I've made the trip before; pay me the money first and lets finish this whisky" he replied.

"I've been a captain for the past ten years and never lost a ship. I've sailed to the new colonies five times, but not always with a human cargo onboard for which I've been chartered for this voyage. However, I have no say in the matter as the ship is owned by the Omedia Shipping Company in Bristol".

Once they had finished their whisky, Hocking called for the bosun to take them below to show them their berths with the crew. As they left his cabin he rose and went out on deck to prepare the ship ready to sail.

From below they could hear orders being shouted on deck as the ropes were heaved in for the ship to be cast off and sharp flapping noises as the sails were hoisted aloft; then they could feel a surge of movement and creaking in the hull as she caught the breeze.

Within the hour the ship was sailing away on the evening tide unbeknown to them that Captain Baker with his soldiers accompanied by Murdo and his men had just arrived in the town making enquiries about them.

Having stowed away their weapons and meagre possessions, they then returned on deck to find out what their duties would be.

Chapter 3 – Journey to the New World

As they sailed up Loch Linnhe, there was a clear night sky as Calum reflected on the unbelievable events of the past few days. He looked over the ship's side and for a moment he thought he saw Siobhan's face smiling back at him through the moon's reflection in the ripples of the waves.

Alastair suddenly interrupted him,

" The bosun wants us heave in some lines from the sails".

A seaman showed them how to do this and so they begun their first task as part of the crew.

They took their turn as part of the watch until the early hours of the morning, then afterwards they went below to sleep in their hammocks, being shown how to hang them up and use them. Their first attempt at getting into them was a disaster but they persevered and once they mastered the technique of mounting and lying in them, they soon fell asleep. For the rest of the night it was only the murmurings and crying of the human cargo that interrupted their sleep.

They awoke swaying in their hammocks and feeling sick. It was the first time they had been to sea. They quickly fell out of their hammocks and made their way up to the deck. It was daylight with a grey sky and no sign of land in sight only the loneliness of the uninviting sea swell. In desperation, they were both sick over the side and lucky for them it was the leeward side with the wind blowing away from the ship. They looked round and saw other passengers vomiting, having been directed by a seaman to the leeward side to avoid any sickness being blown back over the deck.

When they had time to recover they looked around. The ship was listing from side to side in a heavy swell. This was quite normal under full sail said another seaman who told them that she was a brigantine with two masts, the sails square rigged on the foremast only. He gave them each a dry biscuit for the sickness and told them that she had a crew of thirty-four and under full sail she was capable of 6-8 knots. She was called "Beamer" and besides her human cargo, she carried pots and pans; cloth and canvas; spinning wheels and looms; lanterns and candlesticks; crockery, knives and spoons; spades, scythes, axes, saws, hammers and nails; muskets, powder and shot; all for the basic necessities of life in the new colonies.

"How long will it take to reach the New Colonies?" asked Alastair. "Depending on the wind and currents and taking into account the Atlantic weather this time of the year it should take about two months to reach Halifax, Nova Scotia".

Suddenly there was a shout from the bosun.

"Here you two give a hand with these sails."

"Climb up there and help reef those sails" he shouted pointing towards the rigging.

They climbed up the rigging with a certain amount of fear, tightly gripping the ropes as the ship dipped and rose in the waves. Climbing along the main yard they copied what the other riggers were doing, pulling in and rolling up the sail then tying it to the yard with rope. They completed this task after more shouts of instruction from the bosun.

As Calum climbed down the rigging with a sense of relief, it was the first time he saw Frances who had been watching him up in the rigging. She was in amongst a group of families who were now venturing on deck to relieve their sickness and take in the sea air.

For a fleeting moment she caught his eye, then he glanced away preoccupied with images of Siobhan and his children.

"Do you want something to eat?" asked another crewman.

"Aye we're a wee bit peckish" Alastair replied.

They went below to the mess deck and where they were given cheese and biscuit with a jug of ale to wash it down.

As it was an English crew, they were asked to take food and drink down to the hold and speak gaelic to the highland families onboard. As they were soon to find out, there were about sixty of these poor souls onboard, mostly families of various ages, some with young children. All had been forcibly evicted from their crofts and land.

For the next hour Calum and Alastair made a number of journeys from the mess deck to the hold supplying them with cheese, biscuit and fresh water. They comforted a number of the elderly who were either ill or very tired. The hold had an avid smell of vomit and urine and they advised those who hadn't tried it to venture up on deck for fresh air.

They soon gained the confidence of these unfortunate people through their own language and by sharing their own experiences of eviction from Glean Bheag. The families were mainly McDonald.

When they were told the ship's destination was Halifax, Nova Scotia it had no meaning to some of them. As far as they were concerned it could have been the end of the earth as their hearts were back in Scotland.

Captain Hocking on one his rare ventures outside his cabin saw what they were doing and ordered them to take food and drink to the passengers as part of their daily duties. As there was no doctor onboard, he also ordered them to organise medical care to those that were sick.

This they reluctantly agreed too, pointing out to him that they would try their best, neither having had any previous medical experience. They considered that their first priority was to arrange with help, the cleaning up of the sickness, excrement and urine in the hold and to keep it clean for the rest of the voyage. Various men and women from the families came forward and volunteered. The hold then became a hive of activity with the swishing of swabs, clanking of buckets and the noise of scrubbing brushes that they obtained from the bosun.

The young woman in her twenties that Calum had noticed on deck was comforting a number of the sick and elderly and she caught his attention once again. She had long ginger hair that curled down onto her shoulders, an embroidered dress pulled up showing her bare feet and knees. The dress covered a full bosum and shapely body. She was not wearing any jewellery.

She appeared to have a caring and gentle touch as she comforted people.

Calum was driven to speak to her.

"Do you need anything?" he asked.

She turned and faced him and he saw she had an attractive and kindly face with bluish grey eyes.

" All we have are bandages, ointment and water" she replied in a soft voice. "We could do with more medicine".

"I'll see what I can find" said Calum, "Alastair lets go and search for more medicine". As he said this he noticed she was applying a hot poultice to the forehead of an old woman who looked feverish.

"What's your name?" asked Alastair.

"Frances McDonald" she replied with a sensuous smile.

"Where are you from?" he asked.

"Glean Arach, from where we were evicted five days ago by the soldiers. My father was killed in the "45 rebellion" and my mother died when I was twelve which makes me an orphan" she replied.

Calum listened in sadness and anger on hearing her story. He then went with Alastair to see the mate to ask where the medicine chest was kept, telling him of their instructions from Captain Hocking. As it proved, the ship was rather lacking in its supply of medicines, however, they picked up what they could and gave them to Frances.

After a few days, they grew use to the ship's daily routine of watch keeping and the loneliness of sailing in the vast Atlantic Ocean. Besides their duties of caring for the passengers, they became quite adept at climbing the rigging and assisting in reefing and hoisting the sails. They were also taught to repair torn sails and helped with the overall cleaning and painting duties onboard.

For the main part of the voyage along with Frances and her helpers, they had to deal with a number of deaths as the sickness and dying increased amongst the highland families on board. There was only a token celebration of Christmas and the New Year with the crew and families making presents for the children on board. Except for a dram of whisky issued to celebrate Christmas and Hogmanay, there was generally a muted silence amongst the families as they tried to come to terms with the sickness onboard and the loss of their homes and livelihood. Try as they may with the limited medicine available, they could not prevent the deaths of two babies, one middle aged man and four elderly women.

There was also some sickness amongst the crew but not to the same extent. The crew kept themselves apart from the passengers depending on Calum and Alastair to communicate and mingle with them. Those who died were wrapped up in old sailcloth and buried at sea with a prayer being said as they slipped down a plank and over the side into the water.

Then one morning the lookout sighted a floating wreck with broken masts and torn sails. They altered course to intercept and board it from the "Beamer's" longboat. Calum and Alastair volunteered to join the boarding party. As they approached they could see it was damaged so much from the sea that it was no more than a floating hulk. It was heaving and tossing in the waves and the seamen onboard remarked it was the remains of a gaff-rigged ketch. They could distinguish its name as "Lady Jane" with a painted figurehead on its bowsprit of a naked lady with flowing hair that was carved purposely to cover her breasts.

" Well she didn't bring the ship much luck" murmured one of the seamen as they climbed up its torn shrouds spread over its sides.

They heard a scurrying sound as they clambered on deck.

"Watch out for those rats!" the bosun of the longboat shouted.

Calum noticed the rats appeared to be well fed so they must have found food onboard. He then accidentally knocked over a bucket under the fo'c'sle which spun across the deck as the ship rocked and went over the portside.

"That's going to bring you bad luck Highlander" shouted the bosun again.

"Oh don't be so superstitious Wilf" answered one of the seamen.

"You mark my words it will bring him misfortune, OK lets see what we can find below".

"She's got no rudder Wilf ", one of the seamen reported looking over the stern. They searched the ship and except for the rats there was no sign of life. They agreed the crew must have abandoned it as there was no sign of their belongings onboard, only empty hammocks and bunks. The ship's log was also missing from the master's cabin and there was a musty smell of dirty clothing and stale tobacco smoke emanating from inside. Even though the cabin was empty, the occupant whoever he'd been, was long gone.

It was a complete mystery why it had been abandoned and still yet remained afloat. The ravenous rats were eating the only food that was left in the galley and the ship's hold had been emptied.

Alastair thought it was spooky that there was no sign of human life.

"Has she got any seacocks in the hold?" asked the bosun.

"Aye Wilf, we've found them under the remains the grain she was carrying. My God its full of rats down here! Out of the way you bastards!"

Thuds and squeals were heard below as the seaman bashed away killing the rats.

"Open up the seacocks and lets all return to the boat" ordered the bosun.

As the seacocks were opened in the hold there was huge gush of water into the ship and it listed to port. They all scrambled back to the boat and started frantically rowing back to the "Beamer". They had gone no more than two hundred yards when the wreck turned over and sank. It was gone within thirty seconds. As it went under they could see the rats swarming over the side and swimming in the sea.

"Heave away we don't want any of those onboard" ordered the bosun.

They were all relieved to climb the Jacob's ladder to the deck of the "Beamer" and haul the longboat back onboard. The two friends turned round to cast a glance back to where the wreck had been; there was no trace of her nor the rats.

Calum then looked round the deck of the "Beamer". He saw the bosun and the seamen from the longboat gathered in a group and reporting to Captain Hocking. Many of the families were on deck attracted by the event.

"Welcome back" said a soft voice behind him

It was Frances who suddenly stood before him, her long ginger hair shining in the light of the winter morning Her presence and attractiveness took him by surprise.

"I only hope we don't bring more disease onboard, I'll go and wash up below, come on Alastair" he said shyly avoiding her eyes.

During the eighth week of the voyage on a day when the weather was fair and the ship was making a good headway in the Atlantic swell, there was a sudden cry from the look out aloft;

"Ship ahead on the starboard bow" he shouted.

This was accompanied by the mate's order of

"All hands on deck!"

Captain Hocking emerged from his cabin.

"What colours is she flying?" he asked.

"The French tricolour " was the reply.

"Break out the muskets and cutlasses and issue one to each man" he ordered.

The two friends had been informed that there was a colonial war raging in the New World that involved Great Britain, the American settlers and France. They were told the French ship could mean trouble and they quickly went below to retrieve their pistols and dirks from the place where they had conveniently concealed them when they first came aboard.

Besides the muskets and cutlasses being issued, "Beamer" was unarmed and carried no cannon.

"She's about half a league off and closing fast" shouted the lookout again.

There was a frantic haste in the crew to position themselves on the side of the ship that would be boarded. The ship approaching was closer now and could be seen as a French frigate with her cannons bristling from her lower deck.

The two friends along with other able bodied men from the highland families armed themselves and stood alongside the crew. Suddenly a cannon from the French ship fired a shot across their bows.

"Arretez! Heave to!" a voice cried from the French ship, "Or we will sink you".

"Heave to and stand by to repel boarders" ordered Hocking as the French ship came alongside and thumped "Beamer's" gunnels on the starboard side.

Calum caught site of a tall lean man on the deck of the French ship dressed in naval uniform surrounded by his officers. The French crew were also armed and their gun crews were seen to be ready for action.

The sails of both ships fluttered and the yardarms creaked as they heaved to into the wind. There was also a whistling noise in the rigging accompanied by the slopping of waves trapped between the hulls.

As Calum bemused himself with the flapping of the French tricolour flag he was suddenly brought to his senses by the voice of the Captain of the French ship.

"Bonjour, Beamer Capitaine my name is Capitaine Rochelle of frigate "Orleans", we don't mean you and your crew any harm but we are running a blockade to prevent any weapons reaching the English colonies. Can I come aboard and meet with you? If you refuse we will how do you say it, blast you out of the water!

"Aye" answered Hocking anxiously, knowing full well they carried onboard a supply of muskets, powder and shot for the colonies.

A gangplank was placed between the two ships and Rochelle with two of his Lieutenants boarded and was met by Hocking and "Beamer's" Mate who escorted them to the Captain's cabin.

The French captain had an aristocratic and aloof manner about him. He appeared to be in his early thirties a figure of fitness and spoke in an aristocratic manner.

There ensued an icy standoff between the crews of both ships with an anticipation of a fight. The two friends along with the other highland men had made sure the woman and children were concealed below.

Fifteen minutes had passed before the door of the Hocking's cabin opened.

"Oui I will allow you to continue, merci beaucoup for the excellent wine and gift". Rochelle winked at Hocking.

The French party was about to return to their own ship when a distraught Frances appeared on deck and cried out,

"I need assistance, one of women is having a fit, and she needs restraining".

Immediately, three of the highland men went below to help her.

Rochelle and his officers stopped in their tracks and spoke to Hocking.

"You never told me you had women onboard".

"You never asked" was Hocking's reply. Then he quickly thought on his feet and remarked, "We have disease and sickness onboard particularly amongst the women and children".

Rochelle retorted "I've taken a fancy to the one I've just seen and she looks quite healthy and pretty; bring her to me" he instructed one of his Lieutenants.

Both the two friends along with "Beamer's" crew and Hocking became apprehensive and uneasy as one of his French Lieutenants disappeared below and minutes later emerged on deck with Frances.

"Come over here mon petite there's no cause to be afraid".

Frances reluctantly went and stood before him; she felt his beady eyes were undressing her. He circled round her and placed his hands on her thighs. She immediately reacted by slapping his face.

"She has a fight in her like the Coeur de Lion".

"What do you think of her mon braves, do you think she is good for me?" he shouted to his crew. They answered by rattling their cutlasses and striking them on the cannons and shouted back;

"Oui mon Capitaine; are there any more women onboard for us?"

Rochelle addressed his Lieutenant who'd brought Frances up from below.

"Well are there any more like this?"

"Non mon Capitaine the rest are sick with a rash as if they have the plague".

"Sorry to disappoint you mon braves but the rest of the women are sick with the plague" Rochelle shouted back to his crew.

There was murmur of dissatisfaction amongst the French crew as Rochelle turned to Hocking.

"Well I'll claim this one for myself, I look forward to her warming my quarters tonight".

Hocking protested that it could be only a matter of time before Frances and the rest of them fell sick with the plague. He said this as a ploy, knowing full well if there was a fight, his ship was no match for a French man-o-war which had a fighting crew onboard.

Calum took one look at Frances and felt her fright and anxiety at becoming a French mistress.

He addressed Rochelle, "Are you a man of honour which becomes an officer and gentleman?"

"Oui I am" was the reply.

"Then I challenge you to a dual of death for the woman. If you kill me you keep her but if I kill you she stays onboard".

There was a delay in Rochelle's answer.

"Who do I have the pleasure in speaking to? You appear to be impertinent, of miserable disposition and have the appearance of an uncouth peasant".

Calum responded proudly;

"I am Calum Mcdonall latterly from Glean Bheag in the Scottish Highlands and have nothing to lose except my life. I do not have your schooling and training but I have the right to fight and save my fellow country woman from becoming your mistress".

Rochelle eyed Calum up and down.

"What an upstart for a highlander; mon braves shall I kill him?"

"Oui mon Capitaine" shouted his excited crew.

Alistair along with Hocking and his mate pleaded with Calum not to be so foolhardy. They explained that at least Frances had the strength to survive as his mistress until Rochelle grew tired of her. He looked an expert swordsman with a rapier and would give no quarter.

"I don't see you have a sword highland man" remarked Rochelle with a sneer.

"Here have this one". Alastair reluctantly passed him a sword that belonged to Hocking and was similar to a broadsword.

"Beamer's" crew stood firm not allowing any boarding by the Frenchies. Calum took the sword and glanced at Frances. She was sobbing and pleaded to him;

"Please don't fight and have yourself killed on my account, I'm not worth it".

Calum ignored her pleas and faced up to Rochelle who had already drawn his sword. He swished it about in the air practicing cut and thrusts. He was indeed an accomplished swordsman. He also carried a dagger and a pistol that was tucked into his belt. Besides the sword Calum was armed with his father's dirk and pistol.

They faced up to each other on the middle deck. Rochelle made the first thrust with his lighter sword only to be blocked by Calum's heavier blade. Then Rochelle still on the attack feigned a move and managed to nick Calum in the chest through his blouse. Calum retaliated but Rochelle expertly cut a wound in Calum's arm as he deflected his sword thrust.

There was a cry of dismay amongst "Beamer's" crew and a shout of "Vive le Capitaine" by the Frenchies. Calum knew he was being taught a lesson in sword skills and he did not have his targe to fend off the thrusts.

They fought on with Calum receiving further cuts to his torso.

He was bleeding a lot, mainly from deep wounds to his chest.

Then after five minutes, he managed to score with his own thrust and cut Rochelle's face making it bleed.

Hoorah! "Beamer's" crew shouted.

Calum was becoming weaker but some how gathered up his last strength to be fortunately a shade faster than Rochelle who then realised this and sprang to the top of the gangway to gain height advantage. Rochelle then rolled a water cask down the gangway to floor Calum who saw it coming and jumped out of the way just in time before it split open to gush out its contents.

Calum was now loosing a considerable amount of blood from his wounds and was cut again from another sword thrust, which this time cut deep into his shoulder. Rochelle sensed victory and fought his way back down the gangway.

As Calum retreated he slipped over a coil of rope and crashed flat on his back onto the deck.

There was a gasp of awe amongst "Beamer's" crew.

Rochelle closed in for the kill. "Die highlander die!"

At that moment Calum fleetingly looked at Rochelle and glimpsed the evil face of Murdo Mcdonall back in Glean Bheag. He then yelled out in rage the Mcdonall war cry as he looked up at Rochelle who by now had raised his sword for the death thrust. As Rochelle plunged his sword downwards, Calum with a lightening move and renewed strength, clambered headfirst through Rochelles legs, unsheathing his dirk out and stabbed him sharply in the groin. Rochelle gasped in agony as his blood squirted across the deck. Calum then spun him round and using his dirk in a clockwise movement, flicked the sword out of Rochelle's hand.

It landed in front of the French officers who were about to pick it up and return it to Rochelle, when Alastair reacted and stood on it threatening them with his pistol not to move. Rochelle who had blood gushing out from his groin now staggered around in agony trying to get away from Calum. It was no use and he fell on his knees.

Calum now had him at his mercy and disarmed him of his knife and pistol. He stood before Rochelle with his sword and dirk, weakening as he himself had blood pouring from his chest.

Calum raised his sword and plunged it downwards.He purposely stuck it into the deck alongside the prostrate Rochelle.

"I will grant you your life if you honour our agreement on the woman".

"Oui mon brave highlander" painfully gasped Rochelle.

Rochelle was picked up by his officers bleeding and in agony, and carried back to his own ship.

Calum collapsed unconscious from loss of blood and was carried below to have his wounds dressed. A chill wind set in as the French ship made ready to disengage from "Beamer" and sail away.

There were cheers from "Beamer's" crew as the French ship finally heaved way.

Alastair had stayed on deck speaking to Hocking and the ship's mate.

"That was a brave but foolhardy thing your friend did to save the woman, I only hope it doesn't cost him his life" commented Hocking.

"It's a question of fighting for what you believe in and making a stand against injustice and that has been inbred in Calum" remarked Alastair.

"Why did the Frenchies not seize the weapons stored onboard?" he asked.

"Ah its surprising what a bribe of money can do for Rochelle was really operating his own private blockade" answered Hocking.

"Well it saved us from being blasted out of the water" remarked the ship's mate.

Alastair went below to see Calum as "Beamer" renewed her course to the New World. What he saw was a sorry sight with Frances and one of the other highland women tending his injuries. He was still unconscious, with Frances using a fine twine to sew up his wounds while the other woman applied pressure poultices to stop the bleeding.

"Is there anything I can do to help?" he asked Frances.

"Not for the moment thank you Alastair" she replied. "I pray that he survives".

He noticed the other woman was relatively healthy.

"How did you women feign sickness with the plague in front of the French officer?" he asked.

The other woman whose name was Morag replied.

"Just quick thinking, we used makeup to paint spots on our faces and arms".

"We must stop this bleeding" intervened Frances. "Lets sit him up once I have finished stitching his wounds and bind his chest and back with sailcloth".

They did this and made him more comfortable. Calum's ashen face was motionless. The next 24 hours proved crucial, doubts were raised if he would survive. There was a constant stream of visits made by Hocking and his crew to see him as he lay there struggling for his life. The highland families were prevented from seeing him in case of infection. Morag returned to tend the sick amongst the families while Alastair and

Frances remained at his side. From time to time, Frances wiped his head and face to check for any fever.

Calum in his unconscious and near death state hallucinated with flashbacks of his life as a bairn with his parents and as a husband and father to Siobhan and his bairns. He relived the good and bad memories stored in his head with the pleasantries of having a wife and two bairns. As he saw glimpses of his family in his subconscious mind he suddenly realised he could not touch them, as they were all dead. Then he again saw the face of Murdo Mcdonall and with a vengeance it made him regain consciousness.

Before him was not Siobhan but Frances wiping his brow and Alastair smiling by his side said;

"Welcome back Calum, you are in good hands with Frances tending you".

For the next few days Calum drifted in and out of sleep as he fought the pain of his wounds. Frances was constantly beside him except, when she was asked by Morag to go into the hold and tend to the sick. Morag then relieved her and Alastair also made himself available to be beside Calum in case he developed convulsions.

The January weather in the Atlantic with its gales and heavy seas was slowing "Beamer's" progress and one crewman was lost overboard during the reefing of sails. There was a general feeling of relief amongst the crew that except for Calum, they had come through unscathed from their encounter with the French man-o-war.

"Beamer" was now taking a battering in the North Atantic storms with sails and rigging continually being repaired and the crew supplemented by the highlanders, doubling up their watches. The weather changed from driving sleet to snow and with a drop of temperature, they now had to contend with breaking off icicles from the rigging. Due to the cold conditions the helmsman was relieved every hour and each person on board was given hot soup cooked over the galley stove, which consisted of fresh vegetables mixed with salt pork. This was on top of a weekly ration issue of biscuit, salt beef, pease, dried fish, lemon juice, butter and cheese. The men on board including the highlanders also received their ration of ale each day.

By now it was the eleventh week of the voyage some three weeks since the encounter with the French man-of-war.

Calum after many setbacks was gradually recovering his strength and his wounds were slowly healing. This was attributed to France's constant nursing. He was now sitting up and managing to eat and drink by himself.

He looked into her appealing eyes;

"I thank you for looking after me, I think I would have died if you hadn't nursed me, although there were times over the past few weeks when I wished I could have joined my wife and children in death".

"Don't be so foolish I'm sure Siobhan would not have wished it".

"How do you know her name?"

"From talking in your sleep while you were delirious" Frances replied.

"I know all about you".

"How far are we from the colonies?" asked Calum.

"Alastair has had a word with the Captain who reckons we are a few days away from reaching Halifax".

"When will you allow me to get up, I ought to be on my feet before we make landfall?"

"We'll try tomorrow" she replied. "Now get some rest".

The following morning Frances and Alastair helped Calum on deck; he was greeted with applause from the crew. He felt groggy but better for the fresh air in his lungs. Wilf the bosun winked at him and shook his hand.

"I told you a misfortune would happen to you after knocking that bucket off the wreck, anyway pleased to see you up again and its nice to have you back!"

Captain Hocking requested that he and Alastair come to his cabin where he broke out a bottle of French wine.

"To your good health and recovery" Hocking toasted Calum. "We have a lot to thank you for; is your good lady friend outside?" Calum nodded as he sipped his wine.

"Bring her in as I would like to thank her for nursing you and the sick during the voyage".

Alastair obediently went to the door, opened it and asked Frances to come in. She entered the cabin embarrassed not sure of herself and refrained from taking a glass of wine that Hocking had poured out for her.

"I raise my glass to you and thank you for your work in looking after the sick during the voyage" said Hocking. "What are your plans once we reach the colonies?"

Calum and Frances exchanged glances. Her glance lingered on Calum with a sense of apprehension and longing for his answer.

There was a sort of closeness and growing relationship between them; unknowingly to Calum who was still grieving the loss of Siobhan and his children.

"We hope to settle in Nova Scotia and farm; unless Frances has other plans I hope she will stay with us," answered Calum. Alastair nodded in agreement. Her face was aglow as she looked at them with those bluish grey eyes. My God! Thought Calum she is beautiful and she's been so caring to me.

"It will be my pleasure, I don't have any other plans" she softly replied with satisfaction.

"When will we arrive in Halifax?" asked Alastair.

"Weather permitting, we expect to make landfall by tomorrow evening" answered Hocking.

They finished up the wine and Hocking made a final remark to the two friends as they reached the cabin door.

"I knew you were fugitives from justice when I took you on board but you've more than earned your keep, so here is your money back. I hope its enough to give the three of you a good start in the colonies, God bless you!"

They thanked him and gratefully accepted the money, which amounted to twenty guineas. Frances could not contain her excitement and once outside gave them a kiss on the cheek. They then went below to discuss their plans after they arrived in the new colonies.

The following morning there was a buzz of excitement that went through the ship in the anticipation of reaching land. They had started the voyage from Scotland back in early December and it was now the beginning of February 1781 with the coldness of the New Colonies winter at its peak. Alastair and Frances again helped Calum up onto the deck. He was still feeling weak but was definitely feeling better for the fresh air.

The day was dull, overcast and a freshening wind was making the sails flap in a peculiar way as if they knew they were nearing the end of the voyage.

Many of the families were on deck mingling around and deep in conversation about how they were going to settle in the New Colonies. This was momentarily interrupted by a cry from one of the children who was pointing out a bird that had landed on the rigging. It was evident by its plumage that it had came from nearby land and wasn't any type of seabird they had seen on the voyage.

Afternoon came and went, darkness fell and it wasn't until late evening when the lookout shouted that he could see a twinkle of lights and the dark silhouette of land ahead. Sure enough, this was Halifax acknowledged Hocking and his mate. In the darkness they managed to sail into the harbour without a pilot and drop anchor for the night after answering shouts for identification from the shore.

Chapter 4 – The New World

The crew were up early next morning to check for any drift on the anchorage and that the furling of the sails was in order. Most of the families were already on deck, ready for their disembarkation into the longboats that had now come alongside. There was an air of impatience amongst the crew and passengers waiting to go ashore.

Hocking and the ship's mate were checking through a list of the cargo onboard with a man from the shore to see what needed to be unloaded. The day, which was crisp and cold, had certain brightness about it not only from the weather point of view, but also within the ship's crew and passengers that they were relieved to have made landfall. It had been over two months since they started the voyage from Fort William. However, there remained a certain amount of misgivings amongst the disheartened families all of which, had lost everything back in Scotland, but on top of that, some of them had lost family members that had died from illness during the voyage.

Frances and Alastair helped Calum up on deck where they caught their first glimpse of Halifax. From first impression, it was an established settlement consisting of mainly timber houses built to an English style. There were a number of ships berthed along the quayside unloading their cargoes into warehouses. At the far end of the harbour there was a naval dockyard with a ship under repair in the dry dock. Amongst the houses which had smoke from their chimneys curling up into the cold air, they could see people going about their daily business, some pushing carts; others riding in horse drawn carriages. There was a squeaking and crunching sound as these carts and carriages ran over the rutted streets. A huge granite fortress dominated the town.

Some of the families were now transferring into the longboats taking with them their scant belongings and being rowed ashore to a small jetty. Over the next two hours the longboats came and went, unloading the highland families from "Beamer". Some of those who were so sick were helped down the rope ladder and into the boats.

"Its our turn now" remarked Alastair as they picked up their belongings which included the weapons they had with them. Hocking waved farewell to them as they descended down the rope ladder and into the boat. Alastair helped Calum down.

Five minutes later they were ashore and relieved to be on firm ground once again. Their first steps were very unsteady, the body's reaction of having been at sea for the past two months.

They were told by a man on the jetty to walk and follow the other highland families reporting for registration at the Governor's office. Much of the harbour area was a hive of activity with carts busily taking goods from the warehouses. They followed in the wake of the other families and ten minutes later reached the Governor's office. They noticed that the people they passed were better dressed than those working around the harbour.

The men were dressed in tricon hats with flannel shirts under waistcoats and longcoats, with breeches, stockings and buckled shoes on their feet. The women wore tied bonnets on their head, with long frilly dresses under shawls, over stockings and buckled shoes. They all gave a picture of affluence and contentment with their life, occasionally stopping to comment with friends on the appearance of the three of them as they passed by.

Once they arrived outside the governor's office that to them was an auspicious stone built building, they joined the queue of families waiting to give their details.

"What name shall we give?" Calum asked Alastair, "remember we have a price on our head?".

"Why don't you use my surname McDonald, we could be Mr and Mrs Calum McDonald and Alastair could be your brother Alastair McDonald" replied Frances.

The two friends nodded in agreement.

As they came to the front of the queue they could see the man was middle aged, very authoritarian and full of his self-importance. He had a nondescript appearance except for his powdered wig that was obviously making him perspire bringing streaks of powder down onto his narrow temple and puffy cheeks.

"Are you all together?" he asked, as he instructed them to approach the desk.

"Aye" they replied.

"Names?"

"We are Calum, Frances and Alastair McDonald"

"More highlanders! How I have difficulty in spelling gaelic names" he retorted as he wrote down their names with a quill pen.

"Any of you married?"

"I'm married to Calum and this is his brother Alastair" was France's quick reply.

"Just check my spelling of your names if you can and write your ages down here and where you've come from as best as you can along with your signature or mark" he pointed to the parchment.

" Oh I forgot, first language and religion?"

"Gaelic and Protestant for all three of us" replied Alastair. "Second language English".

He scribbled this down and asked,

"Are any of you wanted by the authorities or have a criminal record back in the old country".

All three exchanged glances and unanimously replied "No!"

"Well that seems to be all the information I need; on behalf of the Governor I encourage you to keep together with the other members of your clan and move inland where you can make a settlement together on land previously occupied by French settlers. There you can retain your language and culture. You'll receive provisions and help for the journey. I ought to tell you that the British Government and its military forces are still fighting the colonial militia south of here in the rebel American colonies around New York and in Virginia. We remain loyal to the Crown. Oh! by the way don't I know you from somewhere?" he asked Calum.

"No I've never been to Nova Scotia before" answered Calum.

"No I mean from back in the old country" He pondered over Calum's face for a while then said,

"Oh well, I thought I knew you from somewhere, good luck, next!"

They went outside and joined the rest of the immigrant families. They all wanted to find a church to give thanks for their safe deliverance to the New World. They enquired with a Halifax resident who told them the way to St Pauls Church which suited the families who were all Presbyterian.

Only the two friends refused to go, instead they made their way back to the harbour where they noticed that "Beamer" was now tied up at the quayside and being unloaded. They asked around where they could obtain their own supplies, including guns and ammunition for their journey into the interior. They were told that what they wanted could be obtained cheaply from privateer ships that operated out of Halifax and raided the American colonies.

As they made their enquiries they spotted soldiers dressed in red tunics carrying muskets.

"Oh no redcoats!" exclaimed Calum with a tired voice. "I'm too weak to fight".

"Don't worry you have nothing to fear here" remarked Alastair. The soldiers nodded to them with a friendly grin as they passed by. Calum's reaction was to still keep his hand over his pistol as they passed.

They retraced their steps to meet up with Frances and the rest of the immigrant families who by now would have left the church.

She was waiting outside and told them that all of the families had been offered food and accommodation in the town's meeting hall for the next few days, so they can prepare themselves and gather what they needed for the journey into the interior.

With "Beamer's" crew ashore, the tale of Calum's fight with Rochelle was now being spread around the harbour taverns and they realised that the longer they stayed in the town, there was more of a likelihood of questions being asked about them, especially when it was rumoured that Rochelle had died from his groin injuries. So they decided with France's agreement to leave in advance of the other families.

After a welcome first night's sleep ashore in the meeting hall, the following morning the two friends returned to the harbour and bought as much as they could, provisions and basic necessities for their journey with the money that had been returned by Hocking. They made sure it included muskets, axes, saws, hammers and nails, as they were told wherever they settled there was a fair amount of tree clearance to be carried out, unlike back in the Scottish highlands, which was more of a barren landscape . They were also able to purchase a cart, a few chickens and two milking cows, one of which they hitched up to the loaded cart.

They then made their way back to the meeting hall to pick up Frances. She was inside with a visiting doctor attending to a sick child who had developed a fever.

There had been an overnight frost that had put a white sparkle on the timber roofs. The weather was dry and sunny with a harsh nip in the air. "I think we ought to go now and make the use of the available daylight" said Calum.

"Well I can't do any more here, Morag will you take over?"

"Aye, I hope to see you soon" she answered.

They gave their temporary farewells to the other immigrants who indicated that they would follow them in a few days time once the sick had recovered enough to travel. Calum was then helped up onto the cart and Frances took charge of leading the loose cow while Alastair led the other one that was hitched to the cart.

They passed out of Halifax on a track leading into a surrounding forest. The trees were spruce and fir intermixed with what they later understood as maple. They noticed the occasional grouse and pheasant being disturbed by the creaking of their cart, the cackling of their chickens and the occasional snorting and slivering of their cows.

"I'm told there are white tailed deer, black bear, moose and wildcats in the forest and this is on top of Mi'kmaq Indians which are the native inhabitants of Nova Scotia" remarked Alastair.

"What are they called?" asked Frances.

"Mi'kmaq"

"Any more good news?" asked Calum.

"Oh! the Indians are friendly" answered Alastair.

"What happens if I come up against a black bear? asked Frances.

"Don't allow him to give you a hug!" answered Calum with a laugh.

"You must be getting better with that sense of humour" said Alastair.

They must have travelled about fifteen miles before they decided to make shelter for the night in a small clearing adjacent the track. They first tethered the cows allowing them to graze, cut some wood and lit a fire. Then they cut some spruce branches and built a temporary shelter next to the fire. For a meal, they roasted some meat over the fire and drank boiled milk from a can after milking the cows. With blankets lain on a raised spruce bed they then settled down for the night under the shelter.

It was a cold night with a full moon that produced moving shadows as the trees of the forest swayed in the light wind.

Frances snuggled up to Calum to keep him warm. He fell asleep instantly, as he was still very weak and it had been a hectic day. Then in the early hours of the morning, Alastair was woken by the noise of the chickens cackling and bracken being broken by a large animal. He immediately reached for his musket, jumped to his feet and broke cover from the shelter. He saw in the flickering shadows of the forest one of their cows being stolen by a figure of a man that he could only make out was dressed in animal skins.

"Stop! or I'll shoot!" he shouted.

He waited for the figure to stop.

There was no response so he fired his musket at the running target that must have been some forty yards away. The man fell with a squeal and brought the cow down with him.

Alastair advanced to finish him off. By this time Calum and Frances were on their feet and following. Alastair found the man bleeding from his musket ball that had entered his left shoulder from behind. He turned the man over ready to shoot him with his cocked pistol.

"Don't shoot me" the man gasped in broken English. "I never meant to steal the cow, only borrow it for some milk for my family".

Alastair uncocked his pistol and took a good look at him.

In the moonlight he could see he was an Indian in his forties with long platted hair and a dark tanned face that had prominent features especially his nose. His eyes were brown and mystical. He wore a necklace of beads around his neck and coat was made out of deerskin decorated with a collar of coloured porcupine quills. His trousers were made out of the same skin and tied around his waist with a leather belt that held a tomahawk and hunting knife. He wore moccasins made out of hide on his feet.

"Give me your weapons" ordered Alastair. "Do you understand me?" The Indian nodded and handed him his tomahawk and hunting knife.

Calum and Frances had by now arrived on the scene and Frances knelt down to look at the Indian's injury.

"We'd best get you back to the fire and shelter where I can have a good look at your wound" she said.

The Indian was helped up and taken back to their encampment. Calum retrieved the cow and led it back. The Indian was sat down beside the fire to enable Frances to have a good look at his wound.

"There is a musket ball lodged in your shoulder which must be taken out before it turns septic" she remarked. "Its going to hurt".

He looked at her with his mystical eyes then he stuttered, "Do what you must, by the way my name is Chaku."

"Would you like a swig of whisky to deaden the pain while Frances tries to remove the musket ball?" asked Calum.

"Yes please" he answered painfully.

Calum gave him some whisky in a cup and the Indian winced as Frances poured some of it over the wound as an antiseptic. She used a small thin knife to open it up, so she could prod and locate the lead ball. Sure enough, she found it and extracted it with a pair of metal tweezers.

The Indian showed no emotion but had now passed out, so they quickly laid him on his side for Frances to sow up and bandage his wound. She smeared butter onto a bandage and slightly singed it over the fire so that it would act as an antiseptic before applying it. Calum noticed how expert she had come at sowing wounds; after all, she'd made a good job of his.

After checking his breathing, they laid the Indian inside the shelter and Calum volunteered to remain on guard while the other two slept. He sat in front of the glowing fire pocking its embers for more heat to protect him from the cold with a blanket stretched over his head and shoulders. His musket was at his side.

He dozed intermittently, only to be woken by a draught of cold air and the sobbing of a child. Is that Cailean his youngest! Am I dreaming he thought, no it can't be for he buried him alongside Calum and Siobhan back in Glean Bheag!

He noticed it was coming from somewhere close by in the forest. The sobbing had failed to rouse the others and the Indian was still fast asleep. He picked up his musket and set off in the direction of the child's sobbing. Using the moonlight to see, he trod stealthily through the forest trying to be as quiet as possible and careful he did not tread on twigs that were likely to snap and make a noise. My God the wind on his face was bitterly cold!

He'd gone as far as a pile of dead pine tree branches when he noticed that they had been formed into a shelter. He cocked his musket and crept up to peer inside and to his amazement he found a young Indian squaw huddled together with two children. She had her hand over the mouth of the one who was sobbing. Her eyes met his in terror and she screamed drawing a knife from her clothing. She waved it at him menacing and leapt out of the shelter pushing the children behind her to protect them. She was shaking with fright and the children were hysterical shouting for their father in the bitterly cold.

"I don't mean you any harm" he said as he lowered his musket.

"Do you understand me?" There was no answer as she continued to menace him with her knife. He guessed it was the Indian's family. He gesticulated to her using sign language to indicate her man was with them back at their encampment and offered them drink, food and shelter. He pointed the way back and to the warmth of their fire.

She looked at his him, hesitated and glanced at her children who were by now hanging on her clothing from behind and tearfully looking at him with their hungry eyes. She lowered her knife and grunted in agreement. He hooked the musket over his shoulder and led them back to the encampment. For his own safety before setting off, he made sure she had placed the knife back in the sheaf within her clothing. Both children were old enough to walk on their own and after five minutes they reached the encampment.

By now the screaming and crying had awoke the others as they arrived. The squaw and her children made straight to the Indian who had now regained consciousness. He sat up in pain to hug and kiss them.

"This is my squaw and my two young braves, my wife is called Hitak and my sons are called Chenu and Barak; it was for them I needed the milk". He said.

In the light of the fire Calum now had a good chance to look at them.

Was it a coincidence! Hitak was about the same age as Siobhan and Chenu and Barak looked the same age as his young Calum and Cailean. All three were wore deerskins with moccasins and they looked very cold and hungry. Seeing their state, Frances boiled some milk over the fire and roasted more meat for them.

All seven of them positioned themselves around the fire for warmth, as they ate and drank awaiting for the new day to dawn..

Chaku translated for Hitak as she spoke of their wanderings.

They were from a tribe of Mi'kmaq Indians who had lost their home and lands to white settlers two years ago and they have been surviving by hunting and scavenging ever since..

"Just like us" remarked Alastair who explained to the Indian how they had been evicted from the highland glens in Scotland.

Calum took Frances aside and spoke to her in gaelic so the Indians couldn't understand what they were saying. He had visions of his own dead children in his mind as he said;

"Let's see if we can help them and ask if they want to stay and settle with us, after all they can't carry on living a day to day existence, the children look undernourished and exhausted. We can make use of their knowledge in this wilderness and in return, offer them a future, albeit a humble one with us. What do you think?".

"Calum you have fought for me and saved me from the French, for that I hope I can remain by your side forever; you too have lost everything in tragic circumstances; although our spirits remain in Scotland we've been given the chance of a fresh start, by having the Indian family with us we not only offer them a future but there's a chance that their spirits will look kindly on us until it is our time to join them in death".

He remained mesmerised by her bluish grey eyes as she spoke. She then kissed him on the cheek. This made him blush as he continuued,

"I suppose we better have a word with Alastair to see if he agrees".

He interrupted him from talking to the Indians and called him over to ask his view on the offer to them and his family.

"I agree, lets speak to them about it" he said.

The three of them approached the Indians who by now had become very apprehensive to their presence and future treatment. Hitak passed her knife to Chaku.

"No need for that" said Calum "We've talked amongst our selves and decided to offer you a home with us wherever we end up in this wilderness".

Chaku translated for Hitak and painfully limped to the edge of the clearing, where he stood and looked into the dawn rays of the rising sun. He then started chanting as he stood there. Before long a fully-grown eagle landed on a rock in front of him. It appeared to squawk answers to his chants. He continued chanting for a number of minutes, as he looked skywards then at the eagle. He then returned to them, looked into the flames of the fire and said,

"The spirits of my people tell me to stay and help you".

There was a fluttering of feathers as the eagle flew off.

He translated his decision to Hitak who looked relieved as she hugged the children round her. Alastair handed back the Indian's hunting knife.

"We were told there is land further on that was previously occupied by French settlers when this country was called Acadia. They were expelled when our forces finally defeated the Frenchies in 1755. Do you know where this is?" Alastair asked the Indian.

"I know of a ruined settlement where there's a lake and the land is good and fertile; if we start now we can make it before sunset" he replied. Calum exclaimed to the others;

"Two months ago after the death of my family back in Scotland I placed a curse on Murdo Mcdonall, this curse will remain for ever, but the black clouds that surrounded me at that time have now given way to a fresh dawn with hope and I thank your native spirits that we have become one family".

The men toasted their future with a glass of whisky before preparing themselves for the journey; first feeding the chickens and collecting the eggs they'd laid, milking the cows, and then repacking their belongings on the cart to make room for the injured Indian to lay down. They noticed he had now become feverish and was in pain from the musket shot wound. Calum indicated he was strong enough to walk alongside the cart. They then removed any trace of the overnight encampment before they set off further into the interior.

A light covering of cloud now hid the sun and it looked like snow before long as they continued their way along the forest track. The Indian children became tired after a few hours walking and they were allowed to ride on the cart with their father. They progressed steadily through the forest only making occasional stops for refreshment.

Fleetingly, they caught sight of the occasional deer darting in and out of the undergrowth.

It began to snow by mid afternoon, small flakes at first, then it gradually it turned into a blizzard.

"How much further to the ruined settlement?" Alastair asked the Indian.

"About an hour, then we will come out of the forest and see a lake; the ruined settlement is at its edge," he answered.

"Good as we better get under cover soon."

Over the next half hour the thickness of the snow made it difficult to keep the cart moving and despite harnessing up the other cow, and the Indian and the children jumping off to help push, at times, it took all their strength to keep the wheels moving as they pushed and shoved it along.

The blizzard was now creating a whiteout condition and just as their strength was on the wane, the Indian suddenly shouted, "There it is." As they walked and sunk into the driving snow, Frances and Hitak protected the children from the weather by wrapping them in blankets. Calum was also becoming weak after his exertion in pushing the cart.

They were tired, cold and hungry as they came out of the white covered trees of the forest and entered the settlement. In the greyness of the sky they could distinguish the loch and by now it had turned dark.

The settlement stood out silhouetted in the snow with demolished and decaying timber buildings leaving them open to the weather. They managed to find one timber hut however, that was partly roofed and by ripping out and gathering up pieces of timber they hastily made a temporary shelter inside. Luckily for them the chimney and fireplace in the main room was virtually intact.

Frances lit a fire and started cooking while Hitak prepared a bed for her husband who by now was exhausted. His squaw gave him some herbs to chew for his fever.

"I reckon we can tether the cows here for the night" remarked Alastair, as he and Calum found another ruined building that afforded some protection and comfort for the beasts from the weather. They left them some feed with the hay they had purchased back in Halifax.

After a meal of fried eggs cooked by the women their tiredness caught up with them and they decided to bed down for the night.

Both friends kept their muskets by their sides as they slept soundly and warm in front of the fire. The children snuggled up to their mother.

Just before dawn and as the fire was reduced to its embers, they were woken up by a loud noise coming from the cows and chickens. Alastair was the first to react and leap to his feet, Calum and the Indian followed more slowly due to their wounds. Alastair, musket in hand, was the first to see the wolves. There were five of them, snarling and growling by the cows who were frantically trying to pull and break away from their tethered ropes.

Alastair fired his musket into the air and the wolves scampered off towards the forest.

"We almost lost the cows and chickens to a pack of wolves" he said nervously to Calum and the Indian who by now had joined him standing in the snow.

"They were only dangerous because they were hungry" Chaku remarked.

"Will they come back?" asked Calum.

"Only if we leave the animals where they are, we'd better find them another place tonight that gives them better protection" he answered.

The morning was light and clear after the previous night's snow that had drifted and piled up against the ruined buildings. Frances and Hitak showed the children how to milk the cows but they were more interested in playing snowballs and jumping in and out of the wolves footprints they'd left in the snow.

The cold was intense and everything looked brilliant and sparkling in the sunshine. The loch was partly frozen in towards the shore and its clear waters were of azure blue contrasting with the snow-covered shores. There was a chattering of ducks as they landed and skidded off the ice on the loch.

After eating breakfast, they set about restoring the hut and making it more habitable. This took most of the day even with the help of the women and children. They also moved the cows and chickens into another ruined building that was closer by where they constructed a temporary roof over it and boarded it up to give the animals more protection. Throughout the day they were very busy making a continuous noise as they cut timber into size and nailed it in position.

Their second night in the settlement was spent more comfortable, only an occasional whistling noise could be heard coming from the rafters as the cold wind gusted through them and this was accompanied by the intermittent howl of wolves from the forest.

"We are very low on fresh meat" said Frances the following morning that again turned out to be sunny and cold.

"I think I am well enough to go hunting for you" volunteered Chaku.

"I'll come along with you and you can teach me how to hunt the Indian way. Alastair is properly more useful in staying here and working with the women and children to make the settlement more secure and ready for the immigrant highland families from the "Beamer" that will be following us," exclaimed Calum.

"Yes I suppose so, I expect they are only a few days behind; oh! here is a spare musket for you to use" Alastair turned round and passed it to the Indian.

"You both be careful" commented Frances as she gave Calum a kiss on the cheek. Hitak in turn also gave Chaku a hug.

The two men set off into the forest treading their way through the thick snow covered undergrowth which was illuminated with wandering shafts of sunlight penetrating through the icy tree canopy as their tops swayed backwards and forwards like a pendulum in the wind. As they progressed they knew they were being shadowed by the wolf pack.

Two hours into the forest the Indian stopped and signalled Calum to squat alongside him. They both loaded and cocked their muskets. He whispered to Calum that he could scent a deer ahead and he wanted to stalk it on the downwind side where it could not smell them. Calum followed him as they stealth fully crept further into what seemed to be the blackness of the forest. After ten minutes the Indian again stopped and pointed ahead. In one of the shafts of sunlight the deer could be seen grazing some twenty yards away in a clearing.

The Indian eyed up the target and with a squeeze of the trigger discharged his musket; there was crack and puff of smoke as the weapon recoiled and flew out of the Indian's hands onto the snowy vegetation of the forest. To Calum it was evident that the Indian was relatively inexperienced in handling firearms.

As the smoke cleared they could see the deer lying prostrate on the forest floor.

"Good shot" remarked Calum, "but I see you need some training in the use of firearms".

The Indian retrieved his musket from the snow and made his way to inspect the shot deer. There wasn't a flicker of life in the animal; it lay motionless; it had been shot through the head. As Calum followed, the Indian was suddenly surrounded by the following wolf pack as he stood over the dead deer. The lead wolf was snarling at his heels and the Indian suddenly realised his musket was unloaded. The wolf leapt at him but he managed to deflect it away from his body hitting the wolf with his musket. Tail between his legs the wolf retreated back into the snarling pack; they then all took courage and advanced towards the Indian. Bang! Calum quickly fired his musket and the wolves scampered away into the blackness of the forest.

"Thank you for that, they are very hungry, its very unusual for them to come this close and attack humans" said the Indian..

They reloaded their weapons and tied the dead deer by its legs onto a stout piece of wooden branch. They then lifted each end onto their shoulders. The Indian made sure the weight was taken on his good shoulder.

They retraced their steps back to the settlement; the journey was uneventful, except when they entered another clearing the same eagle that squawked back to the Indian a few days ago again confronted them. It was perched high on a tree branch at the edge of the clearing. Its fluttering wings had dislodged the snow from the branch. The Indian immediately signalled Calum to place the deer down and walked over to meet the eagle. He sat and chanted underneath the bird as it answered him with high-pitched squawks. After a few minutes he returned to Calum and said,

"We must leave some pieces of meat for the wolves, I'll cut off two of its legs for them".

As he used his hunting knife and cut off two of the deer's legs, the lead wolf entered the clearing.

"Don't shoot him!" He shouted to Calum.

The Indian approached the lead wolf that attacked him over the shoot and laid the legs before him. He noticed from the eye contact between the Indian and the wolf there seem to be an understanding between them as the wolf sniffed the meat.

Then in an instant, the wolf picked up one leg and scampered back into the forest then returned to pick the other in order to share them with the rest of the pack that by now were starting to howl in anticipation of a good meal. Calum turned round to see what the eagle's reaction would be; but it wasn't there, it had flown away.

"What was all that about?" asked Calum.

"The eagle speaks for my ancestors and guides me to share my kill with other creatures that are starving".

They picked up the dead deer and resumed their journey back to the settlement arriving back during the late afternoon before it was dark. They were greeted with glee by the others at the prospect of eating fresh venison for the next few days.

"Tomorrow I will show you how to make a bow and arrow for silent hunting" commented the Indian.

"And we will show you how to safely handle a musket" replied Calum. They finished the day in good heart eating a full meal of roasted venison after Hitak had skinned the animal and strangely that night they were undisturbed by the wolves.

Over the next few days, the weather became harsher with another blizzard accompanied with freezing temperatures throughout the day. This prevented any further hunting excursions into the forest so the Indian showed the highlanders how to fish by making a hole through the frozen ice on the loch. The taste of grilled fish made a pleasant change for them instead of eating roast meat.

As promised, the Indian showed them how to make a bow and shoot arrows made out of sapling wood. In exchange, the two friends showed the rest of them including the children how to safely handle firearms. As part of this, the women and children were given target practice in the firing of pistols. The Indian also taught them the art of making a pair of snowshoes for themselves.

After a week, the weather improved enough for Alastair to return to Halifax to meet up with the highland families and guide them to the settlement.

Calum and Chaku decided to go hunting again and this time they decided to take Chenu with them. As they gave their farewells to the women and Barak, Calum felt satisfied that in the circumstances, he was making the best of his new life. He wondered what Siobhan would make of it, but still in his mind nothing could replace his life back in Glean Bheag, but after what had happened there, at least here in the New World he had a future. Deep down he regretted killing those men back in Scotland but this was done at the time in anger and for revenge.

However, his hatred for Murdo Mcdonall remained and if in this instant he'd appeared in front of him, he would have no hesitation to kill him.

They followed a different direction through the forest and after about three hours came out into open land that had signs of previous cultivation and lo and behold, they came upon a ruined farmhouse with outbuildings that must have been vacated by French settlers when like those back in the ruined settlement, they were evicted from Acadia.

The land sloped down into a valley to an estuary of the sea with land just visible on the opposite side. Calum was later to learn that this estuary flowed out to the Bay of Fundy and the far land on the opposite side was later to become New Brunswick. The views were incredible and although the snow covered ground had permafrost this time of the year he felt that the prospects of living there and farming the land looked good.

"Lets have a look at the ruined buildings" he said excitingly. '

"There's a main farmhouse and two outbuildings which can be repaired".

From inspection, they could see that the timber walls of the farmhouse were mainly intact and the out buildings although more derelict; were not beyond repair. He felt in his heart that the place had a sense of warmth and homeliness about it.

"Would you consider making a home here, it looks and feels like a good place for us to settle down from where we can farm and hunt. It is also a good place to bring up the children. What do you think?" he asked Chaku.

Just he spoke, there was a sudden fluttering sound and the familiar eagle flew out of the forest passing over them and down into the valley.

"That's a good omen, yes it will make a good home here" answered the Indian.

In their excitement they realised that Chenu had disappeared while they'd been talking. They searched and found him playing in a frozen burn at the back of the buildings.

"Would you like to live here?" the Indian asked his son in the Mi'kmak language.

There was a delay in his reply, for he was far too preoccupied in breaking off the icicles that had formed on the rocks in the burn.

"I like to live here very much" he replied to his father in Mi'kmak..

"Look I'll stay here for the night while you and Chenu return to the settlement and bring back the others with the animals. I'm sure by now, Alastair would have met up with the other families and guided them to the settlement" he said.

The Indian and his son agreed and set off back to the settlement leaving Calum alone at the farm. He prepared himself for the night by lighting a fire and building a temporary shelter to sleep in. He then feasted on the salt pork and biscuits that he'd brought with him in his satchel.

He realised that it was the first time he'd been alone since the night he'd spent on Beinn Bhreac after his fight with Murdo Mcdonall and his men in Glean Bheag. As he lay there trying to sleep in the shelter next to the fire that warmed the skins and blanket that covered his body, he reflected on his adventures since leaving Scotland. As a man of non-aggression he never thought that hate could fire him up enough to kill his fellow beings. He looked up at the full moon and bright stars and asked for humble forgiveness from the creator of the world. He also pleaded for Siobhan and his children to be safe in the after life and those presently dearest to him to be given protection.

He awoke the following morning to a grey and blustery day of snow showers and set about making one of the outbuildings secure for the cows and providing a pen for the chickens. As he worked he, thought of a name to give to the farm. Why not Bhreac Farm he thought, I'll ask the others when they arrive and see what they think.

The weather had cleared up by late afternoon when he was joined by Alastair and Frances emerging through the snow out of the forest with the cart full of provisions, their belongings and chickens in boxes being pulled along by the two cows.

An ecstatic Frances greeted him with a hug and kiss on the cheek and once they'd looked round, Alastair complemented him on finding such a good place to live. They reported that Chaku and his family had agreed to stay on at the settlement until the spring and show the highlanders the Indian ways of hunting and fishing in harsh conditions.

Over the next few weeks they set about rebuilding the farmhouse using sawn timber logs from the trees they cut down from the forest. They kept to the layout of the farmhouse that consisted of a main room with a fireplace used as a dining/sitting room and kitchen with another small room for washing and three bedrooms. They fitted timber floors to all the rooms and made shutters for the reconstructed windows. The roof was covered with large squares of bark peeled from birch trees and nailed to the rafters. A palisade fence was also constructed around the buildings to protect them from the wild animals, which occasionally came out of the forest.

As respite from their rebuilding programme and as the weather permitted, the two friends alternatively went hunting for fresh meat making sure Frances was not left alone on the farm. They eventually got use to the nightly ritual of wolves howling in the forest.

They also made occasional trips back to the settlement to see how the other families were settling in and how Chaku was teaching them ways and means of survival by taking the men out in turn on hunting parties. The families had decided to call the settlement Strathloch, which they agreed sounded a good name for a settlement next to a loch.

They progressed to a stage where the farmhouse was finished without furniture and this they decided to purchase back in Halifax. They had enough money left to buy a few beds, a table and chairs, along with a quantity of seed potatoes, corn seed and some sheep and a few head of beef cattle.

They decided to wait for Chaku and his family to join them before setting off to Halifax. While they waited they started to rebuild the second outbuilding with the intention of making it the sleeping place for Chaku and his family.

As the snows melted and the days became warmer it wasn't long before Chaku and his family came from Strathloch to the farm.

"Now we are all here I have a suggestion for the farm's name" said Calum.

"What is it?" they asked.

"I would like to call it Bhreac Farm after the highest mountain in Glean Bheag" he answered.

This didn't mean anything to the Indians for they had no understanding of gaelic names. Calum explained to Chaku the tragic story of how he lost his family and ended up sleeping on the snow-covered slopes of Beinn Bhreac. Chaku translated the story to Hitak and the children.

"Being a Mcdonall from the same glen, I think it's a good name" replied Alastair. Frances and the Indians nodded in agreement.

The journey back to Halifax ended up with two trips due to them buying a grey horse and a plough. They also acquired a dog that they called Miky; a terrier that turned out to be excellent for security, warning them of intruding wild animals on the farm.

As spring warmed up the ground they were able to plough and sow the corn seed and plant seed potatoes. The ground proved to be very fertile and in all, as they tended the growing crops and watered them with water from the burn, they became quite content with their livelihood.

By early summer they had finished rebuilding the second outbuilding and Chaku and his family were grateful for they now had their own sleeping accommodation. They were conscious that the Nova Scotian summers were short so they worked hard on hay making during mid-July and in reaping the corn before the end of August. They converted part of the outbuilding that was used to house the cows during the winter to a grain and hay store and another section they changed to keep their crop of potatoes, which they made sure to lift from the ground before the first hard frost.

During the summer they received visits by some of the highland families who had ventured away from Strathloch to explore. They were all made welcome and entertained at Bhreac Farm before they returned to their lochside settlement. One day Calum announced,

"Lets venture down to the sea and see what the fishing is like".

He set off accompanied by Alastair and Chaku who took Chenu along. It was a clear day and from the farm, they could see the coastline ahead as they made their way down the hill over the uneven scrubland. It was one of those summer days when the birds were chirping in a rampant chorus and there was a buzz of insect noises coming from the long grasses. It was indeed a good day to be alive and appreciate the wonder of nature.

After two hours they reached the seashore to be confronted by a wondrous sight of a female black bear standing waist deep in the water, waiting to pounce and catch a salmon from a river flowing into the Bay. On the bank was a young cub following every movement made by its mother.

The bear stood motionless for a few minutes then suddenly pounced into the water with a mighty splash, bringing out a silvery salmon caught in her mouth. The cub tried to copy its mother and stood up snapping its jaws but lost its balance and fell backwards into the water. On seeing the failure of its offspring the mother ripped open the fish and fed some of it to her cub before pulling out another from the water for herself.

The four of them hid behind the riverbank, quietly chuckling to themselves as they lay on their stomachs watching the antics of the bears. They were fascinated by the fishing skills of the mother bear and became so attentive that they failed to hear a noise coming from behind them. Chenu was the first to detect it and tugged his father's arm. They all turned round in panic to see a huge male bear bearing down on them galloping on all fours. Chaku acted instantly,

"Just freeze" he told the others. "Don't use your guns".

The bear was about twenty feet away when Chaku stood up and cried out with a loud shout and excruciating chants. The bear stopped in its tracks then turned away with a grunt and clambered its way down the bank to join its disturbed mate and cub. All three animals then cantered off along the foreshore, the young cub never far away from its mother's side.

"How did you do that?" Alastair asked Chaku.

"Something I learnt from my forefathers" he answered. "He was only protecting his family, his charge was to frighten us off. Any white hunter would have shot him but we Indians are superstitious of killing them, it brings bad luck".

They then made wooden spears to fish themselves and over the next hour they managed to spear seven salmon from the river which was enough to take back to the farm for an evening meal. As they approached the farm they were greeted by the barks of Miky who must have sensed they had brought food back with them and after the women had cooked the salmon, they sat outside to savour the meal and the warm summer evening.

They experienced a bumper crop during their first year unlike anything they were use to back in the highlands where they had to contend with farming a land that was mainly barren. Money was earned by selling grain and potatoes to a trader in Halifax and to the new store that was being established in Strathloch.

On one their trips to Halifax they registered the farm in the name of McDonald and with some of the money they'd earnt they bought a number of sheep, a weaving loom for the women and a quantity of books and writing paper so that during the long winter evenings, Frances could teach Hitak and the children how to read and write. Otherwise the women busied themselves with weaving and mending clothes around the fire.

When the winter finally closed in, the men occupied themselves with hunting and cutting timber. They produced sawn softwood from the spruce and balsam fir and hardwood from the maple trees. As a bye product, wood pulp was made. The wood and pulp was sold to a timber merchant who picked it up from the farm and transported it to Halifax for distribution.

Except for heavy colds and the recurring pain of Calum's wounds that bothered him during the frost and snow, their health was relatively good during the winter of 1782.

The sleeping arrangements in the farmhouse were such that they all had separate bedrooms but Frances longed for the time when she could share hers with Calum.

The following spring, they lost two lambs to the wolves despite Miky's efforts to fight them off. Planting took place once the soil had thawed and the cultivated land was extended to another twenty acres.

At the beginning of May they were invited to Strathloch for a ceilidh to celebrate the McDonald families occupation of the settlement for more than a year. The Indians volunteered to stay at the farm and look after the animals while the others went off to Strathloch. The track between the farm and the settlement was now a well-trodden link through the forest. After walking through a few rain showers it became sunny and warm as they arrived in the settlement about midday. The families who were in a joyous mood of celebration gave them a hearty welcome. The men were dressed in their new McDonald plaids with bonnets and the women and children wore their best clothes made during the past year. There was merriment amongst them when they engaged in conversation, which was a complete change compared to what they felt back on the "Beamer".

One of the buildings was decorated for the ceilidh and there was an air of excitement amongst the children who were playing, running in and out of the building. Alastair found Morag as a partner for the ceilidh. Calum watched them and reckoned they were well suited to each other as they wandered off for a walk along the lochside. Frances changed into her best dress she'd brought with her and put on a perfume hoping it would please Calum.

"How are you Calum have your wounds healed?" one of the highlanders asked.

"They still cause him trouble especially when he's cold and tired" answered Frances glancing at him in adoration.

"Don't worry I can live with it" he retorted.

The ceilidh began in the traditional highland way with the elder of the community telling a story that had been passed down through McDonald history. This had a supernatural theme about it. Then other stories followed, told by other clansmen. During the story telling the women and children remained very quiet and attentive. Topics ranged from those of a mystical nature to those of practical experiences handed down through generations and to new ones that have happened to them since they came to the New World. Once the story telling had finished, it was the turn of telling of riddles and reciting poetry; each person separately making a contribution. Some of the men lit their pipes as they spoke and the room soon became full of tobacco smoke.

As refreshment, there were oatcakes, biscuits, bannocks and scones laid out on a table with ale and whisky for the men and punch and wild berry juice for the women and children.

After the riddles and recitations had finished, it was now early evening and the fiddler struck up a foursome reel. Without hesitation, Frances whisked Calum onto his feet to dance. He was dressed in a deer skin coat and breeches, but protested to her that he looked out of place on the floor with all the tartan plaid around him. Frances ignored his protests and held on to him as he desperately tried to pull away brushing her body close to him.

He felt her breasts against his chest and became aroused with the sweet smell of her perfume. It had an aphrodisiac affect on him as they started to dance. The pupils of their eyes soon became dilated in a fixation of love and he felt an unstoppable desire for her as they twirled around the floor to the music. He was aware that he was becoming mesmerised with the movement of her body and green dress that was hitched up and tied around her waist exposing her shapely stocking legs. As the music played her body moved and swayed to the beat and she constantly smiled at him with her sensuous eyes. It seemed time had no meaning to them and at the end of the dance they collapsed breathlessly into each other's arms. As they sat down he kept his arm around her and gave her a soft hug.

In response, she looked into his eyes and gave him a passionate kiss on the mouth. This brought a tingle down his spine and a rush of blood to his head. As they petted, they became oblivious to their surroundings and knew they wanted each other. Was this due to the whisky he'd been drinking? What about his love for Siobhan? Can he love two people even though one is dead?

With a jolt, he was brought back to reality when Chenu burst through the door in a state of panic. The music stopped and the Indian boy suddenly became the focus of attention. He stood there panting and gasping as his lungs filled with the room's smoky air. The highland children started to stare and pull faces at him, for here was a uninvited Indian boy interrupting their merriment.

Chenu ignored this attention and once he had spotted Calum he made straight over to him.

"Eh, me mama has sent me to speak with yer; soldiers ave come to the farm and urt Papa" he said in broken English. "You'd better come ome".

"Have you come all this way on your own?" Frances asked him.

"Yes" he answered.

"What a brave little warrior you are to have come all this way in the dark".

"If we leave now we can be back at the farm by the time it gets daylight" said Alastair as he made his leave of Morag.

They made their apologies to the McDonald families and hastily departed with Chenu. Frances had no time to change out of her party dress as they hurried back to the farm. It was slower going by night and they stopped a few times to carry Chenu who was now becoming very tired.

As daylight approached they came out of the forest of "Howling Wolves" as they called it. Miky barked as they walked onto the farm. Outside the door to the farmhouse two redcoat soldiers with muskets barred their way. They were challenged as they approached.

"Who are you and what is your business here?" one of them asked pointing his musket at them.

"We live here" replied Calum.

"Oh Joe you'd better tell them inside" he said cocking his musket and keeping it pointed at them.

The soldier called Joe opened the door and went in while the other continued to bar their entrance. He emerged a minute later and said;

"OK you can go in now but leave your weapons out here".

They went inside with Chenu and what they saw in the room made them furious. There were four soldiers facing them with cocked muskets and another with his back to them stooped over Chaku who had been tied to a chair and beaten. The frightened Hitak and Barak were squatted in the corner and being held at gunpoint. Chenu ran across to join his distressed mother and brother.

"What is the meaning of this, how dare you enter our farm without permission?" said Calum enraged after noticing Chaku was unconscious and bleeding about the head.

"Let me ask who you are?" asked the soldier who then turned round to face them. They noticed he wore an officer's uniform but the light shaded his face.

"I'm Calum Mc Eh!........." "Donald" interrupted Frances.

"We own the farm and I'm his wife".

"And you?"

"Alastair McDonald I'm his brother and I also live here".

The officer looked at Alastair and said,

"Do I not know you from somewhere? He paused for a moment. "Let me see, I was in Scotland two years ago hunting down two men called Calum and Alastair Mcdonall". As he said this he stepped out the shadows and into the lamplight. They looked at his face; My god! their faces turned white with horror; it was Captain Baker the redcoat officer who swore back in Glean Bheag to hunt Calum down like an animal.

"I've always had them on my mind since I came here with my regiment last year. They were never found back in Scotland and Murdo Mcdonall reckoned they must have escaped by ship to the New Colonies".

Frances intervened, "You can check back in Halifax, we've registered the farm in our name of McDonald and we have the documents to prove it".

After the initial shock of seeing Captain Baker again Calum recovered his senses and angrily asked'

"Why have you beaten Chaku senseless? Untie him at once the Indians live with us".

"So you know this redskin, I see injun lovers! well he put up a good fight before surrendering once we threatened to kill his squaw and child. I see there's another one of his brats that must have escaped to warn you. Well your injun didn't talk; we couldn't get any information out of him. We thought they were renegades and squatters that must have killed the white settlers on the farm".

"Untie him now" ordered Calum with venom in his voice.

Their eyes met in combat and Baker reached for his pistol.

"Oh I see you are prepared to kill an unarmed man are you! Well if you kill him you'd better be prepared to kill all of us as witnesses" shouted Alastair.

Baker looked away from the challenging stare of Calum and ordered one of his men to untie Chaku. The Indian shook his head and rose, he'd been feigning his unconsciousness and limped across the floor to Hitak and was joined by Frances to attend to his bleeding.

"OK men look's like we've finished here for the moment, lets move on to Strathloch".

As he reached the door he turned and asked,

"Oh by the way, why is the farm called Bhreac Farm? That was the name of the highest mountain back in Glean Bheag".

"Oh it was named after Glean Bhreac in Moidart" answered the quick thinking Frances.

The soldiers left and as they went out Calum made sure they didn't take their own muskets from where they'd left them outside. Within minutes the seven soldiers disappeared into the forest along the track and in the direction of Strathloch. When Calum came back in Hitak and Frances had managed to stop the bleeding from Chaku's head and was comforting the distressed children.

"What are we going to do now?" asked a frantic Alastair. "I'm sure Baker suspects us and who we really are and he's sure to find out from the Mcdonald's in Strathloch".

"Leave to me" Chaku rose and said, "I feel better now; you know there can be strange happenings in the forest".

He collected his musket, powder pouch and tomahawk and moved towards the door.

"I'll go with you" said Calum.

"No the officer redcoat is my quarry, I'll deal with him even if it gives me another headache".

He daubed war paint on his face.

"I'll teach him not to treat us as savages".

With that he opened the door and disappeared after the soldiers.

"What happens if he kills them all, he's quite capable you know; then we're really in trouble?" asked Alastair.

"I have faith in Chaku, I know the special way he hunts" answered Calum with a wink. "I don't think we should go after him".

"It has been a long night lets eat and get some rest" interrupted Frances calmly.

"I'll attend to the animals" volunteered Alastair.

For the first time since they had been at the farm, Frances snuggled up in bed with Calum; there was no lovemaking; he lay by her side wide awake thinking about Captain Baker unable to sleep. He comforted her because she was so distraught and upset over the possibility of Baker finding out the truth, which would have meant Calum and Alastair being arrested and them losing everything. He told her not to worry, for he had every confidence that Baker would be dealt with in the Chaku way. Hitak had said nothing; she was use to Chaku being away on hunting trips and the dangers involved.

By the end of the afternoon Miky's barks and a pounding on the door aroused them. Alastair opened it to find the soldiers back again carrying an unconscious Baker on a stretcher made from tree branches and blankets. The one called Joe who was a Corporal explained;

"Some miles from here on the way to Strathloch we were walking along the track in single file, when there was a sudden rustle of leaves and a cold wind. This alerted us as we felt we were being watched. Then a squawking eagle swooped down on us and as we ducked to avoid it, the Captain looked up and stepped into a hole falling and knocking himself out on a sharp rock. It was rather strange as it was the only rock on the track. We tried to revive him but we think he's in a coma, so we decided to stretcher him back to the farm. If we can rest here for the night and there's no change in his condition by the morning, we'll take him back to the garrison in Halifax and have him treated by the regimental doctor. I'm sorry for what happened here; how is the Injun feeling? I notice he's not around".

"Oh he's off hunting" answered Alastair.

They carried Baker in and placed him on a bed. He had no bodily
reaction or movement as Frances examined him.

"Yes he seems to have a head injury and he's in a coma; in case there's
any change I think we should take it in turn to sit up with him
throughout the night" she said.

Alastair whispered to Calum making sure he was out of earshot of the
soldiers,

"All we can hope for is that when he wakes up he can't remember
anything".

Frances bathed his swollen temple and made sure he was breathing
properly.

"That's all we can do for the moment, I don't have enough skill to
remove any pressure caused by blood clotting".

The soldiers decided to bivouac with their tents outside the farmhouse
for the night. They all waited patiently for any change in Baker. The
friends tried not to show any anxiety in front of the soldiers, but they
were on tenterhooks with worry. The soldiers took it in turn to sit up
with Baker, but there was no change in his condition until just before
dawn when he rolled over in a spasm and coughed up a lot of blood. He
then became motionless and the soldier monitoring him, immediately
called for Frances who did everything to stop the bleeding and revive his
heart, using mouth to mouth resuscitation but after twenty minutes she
reluctantly declared he was dead.

When the friends were given the news their feelings became very
mixed. In one way they were relieved because they felt they were now
free from their past in Scotland, and Baker was the only link. But aside,

although they had a repugnant feeling for the man, they regretted his death. As a soldier they were sure Baker would have preferred to die in battle.

"Does he have any family?" Calum asked Corporal Joe.

"No he's not married, but he's got an illegitimate child by one of the camp followers" he answered.

Frances burst out crying it had all been too much for her.

Calum put his arms round to console her.

"Don't cry my darling you did everything possible".

The soldiers covered Baker with a blanket and placed him on the stretcher for transportation back to their barracks.

"We'll return to Halifax once we've had breakfast" the Corporal said.

Calum didn't hear him; he couldn't believe he'd just called Frances "darling". This was the first time he'd called her that for it had always been reserved for Siobhan.

Alastair went to the byre containing the animals calling Chenu and Barak to help him milk and feed the cows. He decided that work would serve as a good cure for his mixed feelings over Baker's death.

About an hour later, the soldiers departed, after eating breakfast and breaking camp. They slowly made their way off on the two-day journey back to the garrison in Halifax. As they set off they looked a forlorn bunch, as if in retreat stretchering back the dead body of their officer.

By now, Frances had recovered enough to help Hitak prepare their breakfast. It was a sort of pap consisting of oatmeal and water eaten with a spoon being plunged into a bowl of cream. There was an air of mourning amongst them as they ate and they decided to open all the windows and doors to let Baker's spirit escape into the outside world.

To remove their gloom, Calum told them that he'd overheard the soldiers talking about a Peace Treaty which had been signed earlier in the year recognising an Independent United States of America thus ending the Revolutionary War in the Colonies to the south of them. As a result, they said that many of the loyal regiments to the crown were being disbanded in Nova Scotia and the soldiers given land grants. There were also loyalist families coming up to the colony from down south to begin their lives again.

"It's a good thing we had the farm ownership registered in our name" said Alastair.

"Yes except its in the name of McDonald and not Mcdonall. Still when we get married we can change it to Mcdonall" remarked Calum.

This remark startled the rest of them and they looked up in surprise. Frances gasped, as she was about to put a spoon of the pap into her mouth.

Why did he say that? Was it really a proposal? Did he really mean it?

He pondered for a moment looking at Frances admiring the attractive outlines of her features.

"Is that marriage proposal aimed at me? she asked.

"Well my darling I'm certainly not proposing to Alastair!" There without thinking he'd used that word "darling" again.

"Oh my! Yes! Yes! Yes please!"she answered and flung herself across the table and into his arms giving him a hug and a big kiss.

"Congratulations, there's just one problem; where will we find a minister to marry you? There's not one in Strathloch and Halifax is too far to hold a wedding," retorted Alastair.

"We don't need one, we'll make a written statement that we are man and wife and you can witness it. Hitak can cut open our ring fingers and before we exchange rings we can join our them together letting our blood mix".

They were interrupted when the door opened and Chaku entered. He had removed his war paint and looked bright and cheerful. He threw a dead deer onto the table and immediately the Indian children danced around it in celebration of the kill.

"Did you know the soldiers returned here yesterday with the unconscious redcoat officer? asked Alastair.

"Yes" he answered.

"Well fortunately for us he died early this morning and they've taken his body back to Halifax. Did you have anything to do with his accident?"

"As I said before, strange things can happen in the forest" and he looked across at Calum for acknowledgment of what he was saying.

Although further questioned by Alastair, Chaku would say no more on the subject.

The Indians were pleased to hear about Calum's and Frances betrothal and gave them both a necklace of beads as a present.

"We'll make the declaration and exchange rings tomorrow," Calum announced. He went to his jacket which had travelled with him from Scotland to check inside for the gold ring he'd removed from Siobhan's finger as she lay dead back in Glean Bheag. He found it along with pieces of the torn letter that she'd written to the Chief of the Mcdonall Clan. He was suddenly moved by her memory and told everyone that he was going for a walk in the forest.

"I'll come with you" said Frances lovingly.

"No for the moment I prefer to be alone dear".

He went out on the farm and called Miky over to accompany him. His depression had returned when Baker turned up but now he was free with a new love in his heart, however, Siobhan and his children were still on his mind; what would they say? He wrestled with his thoughts as he threw sticks for Miky to retrieve them. He looked up through the forest canopy to wonder at the puffs of cloud rolling across the sky. Yes I'm sure she would tell him to move on and if during his remaining lifetime, some one else were to experience the love he'd given to her, she would approve of it, especially if it results in the birth of further children to replace their Calum and Cailean.

He sat down for a moment and decided that if Frances were to have children by him he would always name the eldest boy Calum and Siobhan's torn letter must be passed down to him and so on…Regardless of time, he looked forward to the day when a Calum Mcdonall of his bloodline returned to Glean Bheag to extract revenge.

As these thoughts ran through his mind his eyelids became very heavy and he developed a tiredness that forced him lie down on the soft grass.

Within minutes he was fast asleep and back in Glean Bheag. There he saw Siobhan and his bairns standing outside their croft waving to him. As he approached through the mist, young Calum and Cailean ran to him and gave him a big hug. Siobhan met him with an embrace that took his breath away. They gave each other a loving kiss that lasted for ages.

"Where have you been?" asked young Calum.

"Oh, on a long journey to the New World far across the sea" he answered.

"What is it like there Papa?" Cailean asked.

"Oh, it's a wild country full of wolves and bears".

"There's also Frances there" said Siobhan.

"How did you know that?" he asked.

"Oh I know everything about you, don't worry she is a good woman and has my blessing".

He tried to touch her again but along with the children she floated through the door and into the croft. As they disappeared, they were waving and blowing kisses to him. He went inside the croft only to find it was completely empty. There was no sign of them or its contents. It was totally barren. He went outside again; there was a feeling of warmth and bright sunlight shining in his eyes. He awoke to find the sun shining down on him through the trees and sat up to find Miky lying alongside him with his ears perched up and sniffing for any sign of danger. He patted him on the head, stretched and got up.

By the height of the sun he reckoned he must have fallen asleep for about an hour. From his dream he knew he had the blessing of Siobhan to marry Frances. He walked back to the farm with renewed vigour; Miky close on his heels. Frances was at the door to meet him.

"Where have you been?" she asked.

"Walking in the forest with my thoughts" he answered.

"Has it affected our love?"

"Oh no, I want to marry you more than ever" he replied.

He explained the dream he'd had in the forest and in response she took his left hand and placed it on her left breast.

"Feel that, it's my heart pounding for you".

They went inside to find Alastair asleep in the chair and the Indians in their quarters. She led him into the bedroom and sat him on the bed.

"I can't wait for tomorrow" she said and started to unbutton her dress before him. He reacted by turning away embarrassed.

"Look at me" she said softly. He turned his head back and became aroused as he watched her continue to unbutton her dress before him.

Slowly she loosened it and let it slip off. She then removed her petticoat to reveal a sleek body silhouetted against the light. She beckoned to him to remove the rest of her undergarments and stood before him naked.

Taking his nervous hands she guided them up and down her body. He felt the softness of her skin and the firmness of her beautifully shaped breasts. He felt between her thighs. This aroused him so much he lost control and was driven to lower her onto the bed and have intercourse with her. It wasn't lust it was the love he felt for her and that was now out of control. With her frantic desire to make love she helped him pull off his clothes and without any sense of order they were scattered all over the floor.

She went to her cupboard and found a bottle of perfume that she poured on his hands and asked him to spread it over her body.

They lay naked on the bed locked together in an embrace of heart felt love. She caressed and kissed his scarred chest and in return, he stroked her sweet breasts as she presented them in front of his face. Then he kissed her nipples with contentment.

When it came to a final unison of their bodies, Calum who'd had experience from his marriage with Siobhan was tender with her because she was a virgin. They lay there afterwards cuddling each other until they heard Alastair wake up and start moving about. They quickly washed and dressed then busied themselves with the household chores.

"I see you've come back from your walk" he said to Calum.

"Yes and I've been thinking about tomorrow, you know I can't read or write".

"Your mark on the Declaration will be sufficient" responded Alastair.

"I'll write it out for us and in time I hope our marriage can be blessed by a Minister from the kirk once they get one in Strathloch" remarked Frances.

She found pen and parchment and after they had consumed a cooked supper of mutton, cabbage and boiled potatoes prepared by Hitak, she settled down and wrote the following Declaration in English;

DECLARATION

"I Calum Mcdonall latterly of Glean Bheag, Scotland, being of sound mind and disposition, hereby take Frances McDonald latterly of Glean Arach, Scotland, to be my legal wife under the present or future marriage laws of Nova Scotia".

This Declaration is made on our Lord's day of 3 May 1783 at Bhreac Farm, Nova Scotia

Signed Calum Mcdonall ....

Signed Frances McDonald....................................

Witnessed by Alastair Mcdonall, latterly of Glean Bheag, Scotland

....

Witnessed by Chaku of the Mi'kmaq tribe.............................

Witnessed by Hitak of the Mi'kmaq tribe.............................

The following day they rose at sunrise and washed their faces in the early morning dew. This was performed as good luck for a fertile marriage. The Indian children also gathered some of the dew in a jug and sprinkled it over the couple's bed to make it fruitful. After breakfast, Frances cut the men's hair and with the help of Hitak made up her own forming ringlets in her long ginger hair. Then she put on the green dress she'd worn at the ceilidh and laid out two newly woven Mcdonall plaids that she'd been keeping as a surprise for Calum and Alastair. After dressing up, the men looked resplendent in their cotton shirts, plaids, stockings and brogues and they gave the appearance of real highland gentlemen as they stood there with their sporrans hanging from their leather belts that held their dirks and pistols.

There was one more surprise for Calum; Alastair presented him Hocking's sword that he'd used in his fight with Rochelle on the "Beamer". Hocking had given it to Alastair after the fight in recognition of Calum's victory and the ship's escape from the French. Alastair had agreed to give it to Calum on his recovery from the injuries he'd sustained.

The Indians were also dressed up in their tribal clothes and ornaments. For the first time Chaku wore eagle feathers in his long hair.

As she stood there, Frances looked very elegant in her green dress that was frilled around the collar and sleeves and matched her ginger ringlets of hair. It had a cream band, which gathered it in round the waist, and the dress came down to just above her ankles exposing her cream stockings and dainty black brogues. The dress without a bodice was a tight fit and showed off her shapely body.

Hand in hand they were led outside the farmhouse to a tree stump surrounded with wild flowers where the parchment had been laid. The Indians held hands and danced around them chanting and making whooping noises. After five minutes they stopped and broke the circle, Hitak stepped forward and cut each of their ring fingers with her hunting knife. As she held their fingers away from their bodies, she took them and opened up the small cuts to make the blood flow. Then chanting, she joined their fingers together so the blood could mix. He lovingly looked at Frances and gave her a kiss. He then placed Siobhan's gold ring on her finger; her response was to place on his one made out of deerhorn that Hitak had made.

"Have you anything to say to each other before you sign the Declaration? asked Alistair.

"Our eyes speak for themselves" Frances answered.

They then picked up the pen and signed the parchment in turns. First, he made his mark, then Frances signed her name along with Alastair who could also read and write. The Indians just made their mark alongside their names.

"You are now married, lets go inside" said Alastair and fired his pistol in the air to celebrate.

Inside Hitak had laid out dishes of meat, potatoes, eggs and oatcakes with butter and cheese. There was whisky for the men and punch for the women and children. The Indians made musical chants and encouraged the newly weds to join in and dance. Over the next few hours they celebrated by joyfully singing and dancing not only for the future of the married couple, but also for what they'd all achieved since coming to Bhreac Farm. The men consumed a good amount of whisky and Alastair was so intoxicated that he let them know of his innermost feelings for Morag.

To extend their celebrations, they decided to send a message to Strathloch and invite the McDonald families to join them the following day. Chaku volunteered to do this and accompanied by Chenu, set off towards the settlement whooping and firing his pistol. The merrymaking went on for the rest of the day and by the time the Indians returned they found them all asleep from exhaustion. Calum was asleep in the arms of

Frances and Alastair was well away snoring on the floor. Barak was cuddled up to his mother; both asleep in one of the chairs.

The following morning, most of the McDonald families from Strathloch turned up bearing various wedding gifts, bottles of rum, a wedding cake, fish and more meat and vegetables. Frances delighted herself by showing them her wedding ring she'd received from Calum. By midday, the newly weds had cut the cake and the feasting resumed at a fast pace; the men danced a highland jig to the pipes and the women chose partners for the reels played on a fiddle.

Alastair was overwhelmed that Morag chose him each time and their relationship seemed to grow closer than ever. The Indians sat in the background bemused by the strange music and dancing happening around them. There were also tunes from a melodeon and one the men played mouth music. When the children became bored they went outside and played hide and seek amongst the outbuildings.

Before dark, the families took leave of them and departed back to Strathloch with a crescendo of guns being fired in the air.

Alastair accompanied Morag back and said he'd return the following day.

After clearing up the aftermath of the feast, the newly weds and the Indians retired to bed; it had certainly been a long and eventful two days.

That night, Calum and Frances honeymooned together in a good conscience that to the outside world they were now married. He promised her that tomorrow he would hitch up the horse and cart and take her for a ride down to the beach in the bay.

The overnight rain left the ground sodden as they set off the following morning with Miky proudly sitting on the back of the decorated cart. Frances took food and drink with them so they could picnic on the beach. Although warm, the day was punctuated with heavy showers but when they arrived at the beach it was bright and sunny. The visibility across the bay was sharp and clear and they could see some people fishing from canoes in the distance. They wondered if they were Indians. "I'll lay out the food and drink" said Frances putting down a cloth on the pebbles.

After feeding the horse that the Indians had named "Grey Cloud", Calum played with Miky throwing sticks into the sea for him to chase and fetch.

Once he became out of breath, he sat down with Frances to eat.

"One day I'll explore the other side of the bay; I believe there's a peninsular of land that connects to it" he said.

"My dear, I'm more interested on us being together today, lets go swimming after we've eaten".

As the warm sun shone on them, they stripped off their clothes and plunged into the rolling waves, emerging from the surface entwined in each other's arms. The rush of cold seawater that tried to separate them was the only obstacle to the closeness of their bodies. Like children they splashed each other ending up laughing and collapsing into the water.

They swam together chasing Miky who was barking and circling around them. When they finally emerged, they collapsed into the frothing surf on the beach and rolled between the waves that broke over their glistening bodies. They lay there, passionately kissing and making love. The buffeting of the waves on their bodies added to the joy of their lovemaking. Miky barked and jumped over them shaking himself dry over their naked bodies believing it was all a game.

Once they'd finished, they washed the wet sand off each other and after drying themselves, they recovered their clothes and dressed.

Miky barked once more, but this time it was a sign of danger. They looked up and saw a party of forty Indians coming towards them. As they drew closer they could see that they were families of Mi'kmaq Indians pulling sleds which carried their possessions. They looked a sorrowful sight that Calum knew only too well.

He made sure his pistol was in his belt before he approached them and spoke to them in a few words of Mi'kmaq that he'd learnt from Chaku. "Where are you from?" he asked.

"We come from the forest back there" one of them answered "But the soldiers in redcoats made us leave".

Frances ascertained there was no danger and saw it was safe to join him. Her command of the Mi'kmaq language was better than his, having learnt much more from Hitak.

"Where are going to make your home now?" she asked.

The Indian spokesman replied pointing in the direction of the coastline on the other side of the bay; "In the big forest over there, where there is no white man. How do you know our language?"

They explained to him about Chaku and his family living on the farm. "Oh we know of Chaku, he is a holy man and descended from a great warrior" he said.

Frances told one of the women to help herself to the rest of the picnic food and share it amongst the children. The Indians thanked them and resumed their journey.

By the time they got back to the farm, Alastair was there with Morag. "I've an announcement to make" he said.

As the rest of them expected, he told them of his intentions to marry Morag at the end of the summer.

"Can she stay here?" he asked.

Calum looked at the faces of the others, Uhm! Morag is Frances friend; and the good news is she is now betrothed to Alastair. Apart from that, the tasks have increased on the farm so much that the two women can do with some extra help he thought; yes going by previous harvests and marketing the animals, they would welcome her with open arms.

"Well it goes without asking you can't be expected to continue to sleep in that large bed all by yourself" he laughed.

Alastair shook his hand to thank him and Morag gave him an affectionate kiss on the cheek.

"My goodness, you do get the attention of women!" Frances quipped. Calum explained to Chaku their encounter with the other members of their tribe.

"The soldiers protect the settlers that come in increasing numbers, our future is bleak unless we learn the ways of the white man" Chaku declared.

That evening he called everyone together to discuss the ownership of the farm.

"We already have the marriage declaration between Frances and myself changing the ownership from McDonald to Mcdonall, but that is not enough now that Alastair and Morag intend to wed; we ought to re-register the papers in Halifax.

 I've have in mind the farm to have a shared ownership of 1/3rd between Frances and myself, Alastair and Morag, and Chaku and Hitak. If we or any of our descendants decide to leave then their share of the farm must be offered up for sale to the others".

Chaku looked surprised, "But we are Indians, we have no rights in the eyes of the white man".

"You do as far as I'm concerned" he answered.

The rest of them nodded in agreement.

"That's settled then, at the end of the summer once Alastair and Morag are married, we'll travel to Halifax and have the proper papers drawn up".

 The rest of the summer passed without incident and they were all occupied with the running of the farm. Once the harvest had been gathered in and on an autumn day just as the leaves were turning yellow, Alastair and Morag signed their Declaration of Marriage. Morag wore a white dress and Alastair his plaid for the occasion. Alastair was overwhelmed with gratitude as the plaided Calum gave him his father's pistol as a wedding present and Morag likewise after receiving a gold brooch from Frances. The Indians again made necklaces of beads to give to them.

 As with Calum and France's marriage, the celebrations lasted over a two-day period with the Strathloch McDonalds being invited to the feasting at the farm. As planned after their marriage, Alastair took both Declarations to Halifax where he passed them to a lawyer who prepared a new ownership agreement for them.

In the early spring of 1784 Calum who was always up at the crack of dawn, was busy in the fields with lambing when the eagle re-appeared. This time there was no Chaku around and the bird settled on the ground infront of him. This time the bird was silent, his head was jolting from side to side eyeing him up and down and he recognised the bird from its markings as the same one that spoke to the Indian.

Is this a warning of something? Why is it not squawking? He wondered. He turned round to see if there was any sign of danger and as quickly as it came it spread its wings and flew away into the forest.

He thought no more of it until he got back to the farmhouse when he told the others of the bird's appearance.

Chaku just grinned and asked him "He was silent then, no squawking?"

"That's correct" he answered.

"Then that's a sign of good news"

"Talking about good news, I've something to announce" declared Frances.

"What is it darling?" asked Calum.

"I'm pregnant with your child" she declared.

He was elated, "Oh my dear what wonderful news!"

"How long have you known are you sure?"

"Aye, I'm quite sure, I've known for the past few weeks"

He rushed over to embrace her and give her a passionate kiss. He sat her down and placed his hand on her stomach,

"To imagine a human life can develop in there, you must take care my dear and not exert yourself from now on; let's celebrate with a glass of wine".

The rest of them congratulated the father and mother to be.

"There you are that's what the eagle came for!" Chaku commented.

Over the next few months he ensured that she rested every day while Morag and Hitak carried out the heavy chores in the house.

Summer quickly passed into autumn and after another good harvest, autumn turned into winter when after a difficult pregnancy, Frances gave birth to a son. He was a big baby with the eyes of his father and the looks and ginger hair of his mother. He grew strong on his mother's breast milk and soon became the centre of attention amongst the women.

Chaku performed a ceremony for the newborn infant, taking him in his arms and lifting him aloft to catch the sunrays, chanting as he held him. Then he handed the baby to his mother and said;

"The spirits are strong inside him, he is destined to have a good and fruitful life". As he said this, they could hear a wolf howling from the forest.

During the following year loyalist families were seen passing by the farm looking for a place to settle. Those visiting the farm from Strathloch and seeing the baby for the first time placed a silver coin in the baby's moneybox for good luck. There was no religious christening for the baby as there was still no minister in Strathloch. Instead, they gathered some morning dew and with it, baptised the child by making a sign of a cross on the baby's forehead. This was to the relief of Morag who had a superstition that until the baby was christened the fairies could abduct the child.

After the spring sowing and lambing in 1785, the friends decided to take time off from the farm and find new markets for their cattle and sheep. As they said farewell to the women young Calum was just beginning to take his first steps in walking. They decided to set out and explore the other settlements along the coast and to find out what was on the other side of the peninsular. The running of the farm was left in the capable hands of the Indians and they took Grey Cloud and Miky along for the journey.

Taking it in turns to ride the horse they travelled west to the coast and turned northwards passing through a scattering of new settlements inhabited by gaelic speaking Scottish immigrants from different clans. Each one they visited were interested in buying fresh beef and mutton from them. Following the shoreline, they passed a group of patrolling militia and crossed a bridge where the mouth of a river flowed into the bay. The weather was cool and sunny giving a sharp visibility and on the other side of the river it wasn't too long before they could see a town in the distance. They found it was called Truro and as they passed through, although it was smaller than Halifax, they noticed it had neatly laid out stone streets with fine timber buildings on each side. The people were dressed in tailored clothes and wigs the same as in Halifax and it must have seemed to the townsfolk, that two men dressed in deerskins with a horse and dog looked out of place travelling down their streets.

They found a place on the outskirts of the town to stable the horse and bed down for the night and once settled they made their way to the local tavern for a meal.

In contrast to the main part of the town it was a dingy place smeared with dirt and grime. Once inside, they looked through the smoke and noise, managing to find an empty table amongst its rough looking clientele. Alastair placed an order with the barman for two plates of stew with bread slices and a glass of ale each.

Just as they settled, through the tobacco smoke eight men approached them and stood around their table. By the way they were dressed they could see they were fur trappers.

"Bonsoir monsieur's, where ave you come from?" one of them asked.

"From a farm more than a days journey from here," answered Alastair.

"Excusez moi we want to know what is bringing you ere?" another of them asked in a threatening voice.

" That's none of your business" intervened Calum.

Miky yapped at the trapper's feet tugging at his deerskin trousers, when with a sudden jerk, he gave the dog a violent kick which sent him flying across the room squealing and yelping in pain.

"Why did you do that to the poor animal?" raged Calum standing up to challenge him.

"Oh excusez moi, ow do you say, its none of your business!" the trapper sarcastically replied with a snear.

Calum reached for his pistol and dirk.

"Mon Dieu! It's the highlander that killed mon capitaine" one of them exclaimed. "Keep away from him he is extremely dangerous!"

The dog returned to his master's side and continued to growl.

The trappers backed away and the one that recognised Calum was seen telling the others how he'd been a sailor on a French man-of-war during the winter of 1780 and witnessed the dual between Rochelle and the highlander on the "Beamer". There were the occasional mutterings and pointing of fingers at them but for the next hour they were left in peace to enjoy their meal and drink. When they rose to leave the inn at the end of the evening, they made sure their hands were kept over their pistols. Outside they feigned their walk to the stables as if they were heading back into the town and then double backed to make sure they were not being followed.

They spent an uneasy night amongst the hay and started out early the next morning travelling along a track further along the peninsular. The day was warm with a thick mist making the visibility less than a hundred yards. As they travelled, they talked over the previous evening's events and decided to keep a watchful eye out for the trappers.

They knew that the trappers could seek revenge for killing one their countrymen, albeit in fair combat and they both knew that with changed circumstances, they now had dependents and a secure life. The last thing they wanted was to end up fighting a band of ruffian fur trappers.

By mid morning, they'd travelled ten miles over a tree clad rocky terrain crossing the Cobequid Mountains, the mist only lifting in places. Miky was ahead of them when they heard him barking in the mist; then there was a thud and he started squealing; then there was silence. They exchanged glances with each other and primed their muskets.

Alastair who was mounted on Grey Cloud cantered forward to investigate. He'd gone about fifty yards when he noticed the dog lying alongside the forest track covered in blood. He dismounted and walked over to the poor dog who lay motionless to see if he were still alive. The dog whimpered as he stroked him.

Thump! He was suddenly hit on the head from behind and passed out.

Before he lost consciousness he caught a blurred glimpse of trappers standing over him. The trappers started to disarm him and search through his clothes for valuables, but before they could finish, Calum was now on the scene screaming his clan warcry then ordered them;

"Stand away from him you Frenchies and put your weapons down under that tree. The first person that raises his musket or goes for his pistol is dead meat! I mean it!".

"Oh highlander we are eight and you are one. It is you; oh ow do you say it at a disadvantage. You ave two shots for eight people. I think its you that are dead meat nes pas! said the snearing trapper.

"Was it you that hurt my dog again?"

"Le chien, Oui".

"Well it's going to be you that gets the first shot! Now who's going to be the second to die?"

There was chilling venom and a streak of determination in his voice for he was now fired up as he'd been with Murdo Mcdonall.

With a lightening movement the snearing trapper pulled out his pistol and fired it at him.

Bang! he simultaneously discharged his pistol in reply.

He suffered a graze to his neck but the trapper was shot in the stomach and healed over backwards onto the ground.

He composed himself. "Now who's next?"

There was no need as one by one, the rest of them laid down their weapons underneath the tree. By now, Alastair had recovered his senses and rose to his feet clutching his musket and pistol.

The last one to lay down his guns was the ex-sailor who bent over and fumbled for something inside his coat, then he suddenly turned and before Calum could react, threw a knife which struck him in his chest. He then picked up his pistol to finish him off.

Bang! There was a shot and the Frenchman fell back dead.

Alastair stood there with a white face and in shock holding a smoking musket. It was the first person he'd ever killed.

Calum staggered around still holding his loaded pistol with blood pouring from his chest. For the rest of the trappers it was enough by now and they raised their hands aloft.

"Pick up your friends and take them away" Alastair retorted.

Frightened for their life they obeyed and two of them helped the snearing one to his feet with his hands still clutching a wounded stomach. Another two of them picked up the limp body of the dead sailor.

At that moment, redcoat soldiers appeared out of the forest with loaded muskets.

"I see you've had a run in with these cutthroats; Ok we'll take over from here" their officer said.

Looking at Calum he said; "I see you are wounded, medic attend to him then the trapper. Oh by the way I'm Lieutenant Mcdonall, don't I know you from somewhere?"

He then spoke in gaelic so the other soldiers couldn't understand.

"You are Calum and Alastair Mcdonall from Glean Bheag back in Scotland, correct?"

"Aye" answered Calum reluctantly expecting the worse.

"I'm honoured to meet you both, I was there five years ago when you both escaped after your family were murdered by Murdo and his henchmen. My family was also evicted from the glean a month later and we also made it to Nova Scotia where I joined the military. Don't worry we'll take these cutthroats in; they are wanted for other murders. Where have you settled in Nova Scotia?".

There was apprehension on their faces.

"Don't worry your secret of being fugitives is safe with me, after all my family suffered as well".

"At Bhreac farm near Strathloch" answered Alastair who had by now recovered enough to join in the conversation.

"I'll make a note of it and offer my services if you ever need help. How did you become involved with this riffraff?"

Alastair explained their run in with the trappers at the inn and how Calum had been recognised for his fight with Rochelle on the "Beamer". The medic carefully removed the knife from his chest and bound the wound with bandages. He was lucky for it not to have penetrated his lungs or heart.

Once this was complete, the Lieutenant walked up to him.

"Calum let me shake your hand for the future, your friend tells me you have a new wife and child, may the rest of your life be blessed with good fortune, you certainly deserve it". He then saluted him. "To the memory of Glean Bheag!"

"Always" answered the two friends.

The medic managed by now to stop the bleeding from the trapper's stomach and they carefully placed him on a stretcher for transit. Another two soldiers picked up the dead body of the sailor.

The rest of the trappers were manacled and led off in single file escorted by the soldiers. Lieutenant Mcdonall bade his farewell and the party went off into the mist that enveloped them within minutes. They treated Miky's wound and found Grey Cloud grazing a few hundred yards away after his initial stampede during the gunfire.

Calum was groggy but able to walk so they decided to continue with their journey. The next inhabited place they found was a town called Amherst that they came upon late in the afternoon. The weather still remained misty as they walked through its streets; again, to find a place to stay and stable the horse overnight.

During the next few days they crossed the Petitcodiac river and travelled southwards along the north side of the Bay of Fundy. At Parrtown and Carleton at the mouth of the Saint John river that was later that year to become Saint John, they saw the spectacular sight of the reversing falls and witnessed the whales that swam in the Bay during the summer months feeding on the sea food churned up twice a day on the gigantic tides. From Mi'kmaq lore they knew that it was a giant whale who had angered the Glooscap and created such a splash with his tail to cause the gigantic tidal surge.

They found out that the land they'd been on since leaving Amherst was now administered as a separate province called New Brunswick and at Parrtown approximately 7000 refugee loyalists in 1783 had landed in the harbour from a fleet of twenty ships sailing from New York after the end of the Colonial War.

The main industry of the town consisted of shipbuilding and lumber and they were told that arrangements had been made for provincial elections to be held later in the year. By now, having experienced the hustle and busy traits of four towns that to them were unexpected, they longed to return to the wilderness and resume hunting and farming for their families. They retraced their way back to Bhreac Farm travelling a different route camping in the forest to avoid the towns, but visiting different settlements on the way. They'd been away exactly two weeks when they spotted Chaku and the Indian children working in the fields. Miky barked in recognition as they came in view of the farmhouse. The women hugged and kissed them as if they were soldiers returning from war. Young Calum was encouraged by his mother to take a few tottering steps towards his father before being scooped up in his arms and cuddled.

"Why is your chest bandaged?" observed Frances.

He told them of their encounter with the trappers and their meeting with Lieutenant Mcdonall.

"I let you out of my sight for a short while and this happens. You know your body can't take many more knife wounds" she exclaimed.

When Chaku and the Indian children arrived home from the fields there was much conversation over the meal table that evening with both of them talking about the things they'd experienced and seen.

As it turned out Calum's chest wound quickly healed within a month but was an added scar to the sword wounds he'd received on "Beamer". The next few years were uneventful, as they concentrated on making a living from the farm. The Indian children grew up to be young braves retaining their culture of hunting, fishing and spiritual beliefs alongside learning farming and language skills and experiencing highland customs as being part of a highlander's family. Frances and Morag continued with the Indian's education into the white man's ways to help them cope with their changed life as a minority race in their homeland.

Young Calum was a chirpy toddler continually showing affection by climbing on his father's lap and asking to be bounced up and down. He was also determined on having stories read out to him. These were read by his mother from English books, but the ones told to him by his father and Uncle Alastair were in gaelic, so he became bi-lingual speaking and understanding English and Gaelic with a smattering of the Mi'kmaq language from the Indians.

His favourite toys were a wooden trolley made by Alastair which he constantly drove into the furniture and a rocking horse falling off until he mastered his balance. Falling off chairs and the dinning table were common and a metal guard had to be placed around the log fire for his own safety.

After his toddler stage he grew up to be an athletic and strong boy with the brains of his mother and the determination and vigour of his father.

He was artistic too and painted in oils producing excellent landscapes and their portraits on canvas. He was always at the side of his father during their hunting trips and when there was work on the farm.

Alastair and Morag also had children; first a boy called Ross and then a girl called Christina. They were born in 1787 and 1789. It was the first girl born at Bhreac Farm and this resulted in much joyous celebration.

By the end of the decade Strathloch had developed into a thriving community with shops, a kirk with a long awaited minister and a school.

Both highland families travelled to Strathloch to have their marriages finally blessed and children baptised by the kirk. This was done on the request of the women and with the future of the chidren in mind, The men reluctantly agreeing as they had no faith in the kirk which had failed to intervene back in Glean Bheag with the clearances.

One day during the summer of 1790, Chaku came back from a hunting trip and announced;

"I've had a visit from the eagle today, I have to leave to make a stand for my people across there" he pointed in the direction of New Brunswick land.

"They are being driven out of their hunting and fishing grounds by the settlers".

"I'll go with you" Calum volunteered.

"No, from you I have learnt the ways of the white man and I thank you all; I must help them the Chaku way".

After a few hours spent consoling his family in the outhouse where from time to time they could hear spurts of chanting and wailing, he emerged and bade them farewell.

He had eagle feathers in his hair once more and carried his musket, powder pouch and ammunition along with his bow and arrows, tomahawk and hunting knife tucked into his belt. He looked a formidable warrior as he embraced his wife and the rest of them. When it came to the turn of Calum he pressed a bear's claw into his hand. "Keep this on the farm it will bring you all good luck".

He then made off with his two sons who said they would accompany him as far the coast. He waved back to them before disappearing into the trees. His young braves returned before evening looking rather dejected. Did they sense something with their father's behaviour?

Unbeknown to them at the time, it was the last time they saw Chaku; he was never seen again.

The bear claw took pride of place above the fireplace.

Six weeks passed without Chaku returning and just as Calum was about to set off with the young braves in search of him, Lieutenant Mcdonall and his men visited the farm. When asked if he knew anything about Chaku, Lieutenant Mcdonall said they had just come from New Brunswick and related a story about a M'ikmaq Indian who during the past month had stood before the Provincial Assembly in Frederickton and spoke in eloquent English putting the case for his people not to be evicted from their traditional fishing and hunting grounds. Evidently, a group of white miners had moved in on their land to mine lead. He also obtained an audience with the Governor and in the outcome won his people's case.

Soldiers were instructed to remove the miners, but a few gave the soldiers the slip and returned to the mine they had dug in a hillside. When they were inside, the roof caved in crushing and killing them just as the soldiers arrived to eject them. One eye witness said that as the roof collapsed with a billow of dust blowing out of the entrance a squawking eagle flew out of the mine.

"By your description, I believe this Indian must have been Chaku. What happened to him?" Calum asked the Lieutenant.

"It was reported that he was murdered for revenge by a band of trappers and miners. At the site of the murder they found seven bodies of the band, but the body of the Indian was never found; he just vanished".

The Indians listened attentively to what the officer had to say, then on hearing of Chaku's death they started wailing with tears in their eyes. Hitak was comforted by Frances and the boys by the two friends.

"Your father was a great warrior and we will remember him forever. He brought you both up well and taught you the traditions of your people that you must never forget" stated Alastair.

After a glass of ale the Lieutenant and his platoon departed leaving them to digest the unexpected news he'd given them.

That evening was tinged with extreme sadness for the death of Chaku not only meant the loss of a dear friend to the highlanders but to them it was a member of the family. As the sun set that evening they looked at the silhouettes of the forest against the red glow of the sky and chanted a lament along with the Indians as the wolves begun to howl.

It was the end of the Chaku chapter in their lives and they felt honoured to have known him and the mystery that surrounded him. From now on each time they saw an eagle in the forest they wondered if it had any connection with Chaku.

After Chaku's death there followed a period when the Indian boys grew in stature and matured into fine warriors. Their father would have been very proud of them. They taught young Calum the Indian ways of hunting and found time to play with Ross and Christina. The children's favourite game was hide and seek in the haystore and riding the cart.

Calum had purchased a crochet game which they played on the trimmed grass outside the farmhouse. Morag turned out to be this game's expert player winning most of the matches.

The 1790's were a peaceful and pleasant period on the farm that enriched the highland and Indian families with a plentiful produce of meat, eggs, milk, cereal crops and with the sale of lumber cut from the forest.

The highland families regularly attended the annual gatherings in Strathloch dressed in their plaids where they took part in "putting the stone" and "tossing the caber"; the younger members competing in a running race alongside the loch. The gatherings always ended in a ceilidh in the evening. Young Calum excelled in "tossing the caber" event after practising on the farm with cut logs. His father reigned supreme in the broadsword-fighting contest.

The children received home education from Frances but were taken one day a week to the new school in Strathloch.

Although happy with one son, try as they could, Frances failed to become pregnant again. This however, did not alter the love they had for each other.

One day, a piano was delivered to the farm. This was purchased by Alastair from Truro and brought music to their lives especially during the long winter evenings. Morag knew how to play it and decided to teach the children. One winter's evening after she'd spent playing it in the afternoon and scribbling down notes on parchment, she said;

"Hear this, I've composed a reel that I've called Ben Bhreac".

As she played it Frances jerked Calum onto his feet and danced around the floor.

"My you've composed a fine reel" reacted Alastair.

"Thank you my dear, I've composed it to remind us all of our happy times here".

Ross and Christina tried to copy the dance movements but fell down giggling on the floor.

In enjoying the growing up of their children it proved to be the most settled times of their lives since arriving in the New World.

An event happened in 1799 that they never thought was possible.

Young Calum developed a cold that prevented him from accompanying his father on a hunting trip. It was autumn just after the harvest had been completed.

Miky had died from old age some years earlier and a young Labrador called Brandy now accompanied Calum. Alastair and the rest of the males were busy preparing the farm for the winter.

Calum had decided to hunt further into the interior but failed to return after four days. Frances was frantic with worry and asked the men to search for him.

"He told me he would be away for a two day's at the most" she said. "Don't worry we'll find him, I'm sure he'll be all right" responded Alastair.

What they didn't know was Calum on his return to the farm had suddenly felt ill and collapsed. His old sword wounds were causing him grief and he had a fuzzy feeling with pains in his head. As lay on the ground he realised he could not move his right arm or leg. His body was totally paralysed on the right side and he found it difficult to call Brandy. He knew what he wanted to say to the dog but the words would not come out. He lay there unable to get up with his musket by his side and pistol in his good hand for protection.

From the intense pain in his head, he wavered into a semi – conscious state as he grew cold lying on the damp ground. Brandy sensed his master's demise and lay on top of him to keep him warm. His mind wandered back to Glean Bheag and found himself greeting his mother and father; then as he walked further on there were images of Siobhan and the bairns again rushing to meet him. From a distance he saw Chaku and wondered what he was doing in the glean. These are all dead people he thought and he'd experienced this feeling before while in a state of near death after his fight with Rochelle onboard "Beamer".

In his mind there were also blurred pictures of Rochelle and Captain Baker, then he saw the sneering trapper once again. He thought the way out of this trauma was to think of Murdo Mcdonall; this had worked on the "Beamer". As hard as he tried all he could visualise were Frances and young Calum's happy faces.

There was now a bright light enveloping him and he felt the life force in his body faltering. After a moment he had the peaceful sensation of floating with all the pain gone.

They found him the following day by Barak recognising the howling sound of Brandy. When they came upon the scene the dog was lying by his dead master's side and from the surrounding footprints there was evidence that he'd chased off some wolves who were interested in the dead carcases of the rabbits that Calum had shot.

They were shocked and dumbfounded seeing Calum's prostrate body lying under a tree where he'd obviously dragged himself for cover from the elements.

Between them they carefully picked him up and carried his dead body back to the farm. On seeing him Frances became hysterical and in a state of severe shock. As best as they could, the tearful Morag and Hitak placated her.

"Oh why did he have to die like this and alone, after all that he's been through" she screamed.

Young Calum sat sobbing in the corner.

"Its all my fault, none of this would have happened if I'd been with him" he said with tears in his eyes.

"Its nobody's fault don't blame yourself" replied Alastair.

He placed his arm round Frances and spoke soothingly;

"He was my boyhood friend and we've been through a lot together. Except for his old sword injuries he was fit, as one can be for a fifty four year old man. I'm not sure what caused his death but from the signs on the ground where he had managed to drag himself under a tree, the marks indicated that he was paralysed on the right side of his body. He was to me a beacon of righteousness throughout his life and you could depend on him whenever there was trouble, but his spirit will not finally rest until it has revenge for the murder of his first wife and children. We must accept our lives for what we make of them; in a number of circumstances there is no pre-warning of death which can be sudden and final, leaving our loved ones devastated with grief".

His eyes became watery and bloodshot as he said this.

Young Calum rose to comfort his mother.

"Don't worry, I promised Papa that I'll look after you if anything happened to him" he said.

"He elped us when we ad nowhere to go and our spirits will onour im as in life and in death" interrupted Hitak in broken English who spoke with some dignity.

Alastair with the help of young Calum made a coffin out of the lumber on the farm and Calum's dead body was placed inside and laid out in their bedroom with his sword and dirk laid across his chest. Frances kept a vigil by his side. When she became tired one of the others took turns to maintain the vigil. The room was shrouded in white linen with the curtains drawn and the mirror and paintings covered over. A message was sent to Strathloch informing the highland community of Calum's death using Barak as a courier so arrangements could be made for his funeral.

On the day of the funeral there seemed to be the whole population of Strathloch that turned out; so was the amount of respect that Calum held within that community. Each person queued to touch his body in the open coffin and some placed fragrant sprigs of wild lavender on him. A few kissed his cheek or temple.

On the stroke of midday, Frances dressed in a black dress, presented his sword and dirk to young Calum who had on his father's plaid with black ribbons flowing from the clasp and the coffin was closed. It was then placed on the cart drawn by Grey Cloud and with Frances and her son on each side of it Alastair with his family followed behind with the Indians chanting. The funeral procession of some hundred and thirty people then slowly walked off to the burial place set on a hillock on the farm.

As the coffin was lowered into the freshly dug grave on the edge of the forest amongst a clump of trees young Calum experienced a tingle in the back of his neck and desperately clung to his grieving mother as she threw a bunch of wild flowers into the hole. A piper with black ribbons tied to his bagpipes played a Mcdonall lament but paused when the minister said a short prayer. The funeral cortage slowly paraded past the grave pausing to pay their last respects at the graveside, then they all made their way back to the farmhouse for the wake.

A familiar noise made young Calum stop and look back with his mother. They saw a squawking eagle sitting on the grave. The Indians had also heard the noise and looked round.

"It's a sign of respect for him by our spirits" declared Chenu.

That night the howling of wolves in the forest seemed to be louder than usual.

Chapter 5 - New World Descendants

"Aye, that's my family tree and I come from a long line of Calum Mcdonalls from way back in the 18th century when the first Calum came across to Canada".

It was 1913 and a fifth generation Calum Mcdonall aged twenty-seven stood proudly in the parlour of Bhreac Farm showing his guests the framed family tree on the wall.

"Let me see now you asked about the first Calum who married Frances McDonald and had a son of the same name. By tradition the oldest son in the family is called Calum ". He pointed to the family tree that was in a frame on the wall which showed, starting with the first Calum;

MCDONNALL FAMILY TREE
FROM 1744 UNTIL PRESENT

Calum Mcdonall b1744 d1799 m Siobhan Mcdonall b1752 d1780

I

Calum b1774 d1780

I

Cailean b1776 d1780

m Frances McDonald d1814

I

Calum b1784 d1820 m Beatrice ld b1786 d1858

```
_____I_____
I                        I                    I
Calum b1809 d1889        I          Flora b1814 d1888
                         I
```

Alexander b1811d1873 m Lucinda Graham b1814 d1880

```
_____ I _____
I                        I                     I
Calum b1833 d1833        I            Robert b1845 d1898
                         I          m Catriona Cameron b1852 d1907
                         I                              I
                         I                              I
Ian b1834 d1910 m Fiona McDonald b 1832 d1883           I
                         I                              I
                         I                              I
Norman b1854 d1903 m Natasha Schreuder b1853 d 1911     I
                         I                              I
              Calum b1886                      Fiona b1899
```

"Aye that's him, he was the first to settle here. That's his sword and dirk on the wall."

"I understand the farm was first registered under the name of McDonald" said one of the guests.

"Aye that's correct, it was because Calum and Alastair were fugitives and didn't want their real names disclosed; but after a few years they changed it to Mcdonall as soon as they knew they were safe here in Canada. Incidentally, we still have the descendants of Alastair and the Indians living on the farm".

He explained that the second Calum had fought with Barak one of the Indians from the farm during the 1812-14 war that broke out between the United States and the British in Canada. He told them that they joined up with Colonel Robert McDonall and his men and helped with the building of Fort Drummond on Drummond Island, Chippewa County, Michigan,USA. After the war was over, they returned to the farm for it was important for Calum to be with his mother who had never got over his father's death. He continued,

"Mind you when Calum married Beatrice who had three children she was mighty proud of her grandchildren. She died in 1814 after a short illness clutching a portrait of his father. There was much sadness at the farm when she passed away. Then in 1820 Calum was struck down with acute appendicitis from which he also died".

Pointing to the family tree again.

"The third Calum was a bachelor who spent his whole life working on the farm with his spinster sister Flora building up the lumber business. However, the second son Alexander also had three children and their first child, who was the fourth Calum sadly passed away in 1833 having caught pneumonia one month after he was born".

"Besides the weapons on the wall do have any other mementos from Scotland?" one of them asked.

He opened a drawer in the sideboard and produced an envelope.

"In this envelope is a torn letter dated September 27,1780 from Scotland that has a historical significance within the family and which has been stuck back together. If for any reason, a member of the family were to visit Scotland then they must take it with them. Before you ask me why? It is a secret held within the family. Finally, as you can see I'm the only child of Norman and Natasha but I do have a younger niece Fiona. Now I'm sure you must be bored with hearing our family history, what about something to eat and drink before you leave?".

A year later, when the First World War broke out in Europe, Calum volunteered and joined the Canadian Black Watch Highlanders. He took the torn letter with him thinking he might have a chance to visit or serve in Scotland while abroad. Unfortunately, after six months of training in Canada, his company was posted straight away to the western front in Northern France as part of the Canadian forces.

Before leaving he met a young Halifax girl named Sinead and became engaged to her on the night before his departure. She pleaded with him not to go but realised his mind was made up to serve his country.

"I love you Calum, please come back and marry me" she said to him.

"Aye that I will my love, the war will be over in a year".

How wrong that proved to be, on arrival in France the regiment disembarked at Calais and was straight away ordered to march to the front. It was the autumn of 1915 when trench warfare had well and truly been established and had reached stalemate between the opposing armies.

There was a cold chill in the wind as they marched along the tree-lined roads stamping over yellow carpets of damp autumn leaves. Then it started to rain.

"Close up at the rear!" the company sergeant shouted.

Their three hours of marching was only interrupted with brief fallouts for mugs of tea brewed up in the rain under sheets of tarpaulin.

His first taste of war was presented by lines of wounded soldiers passing them in the gloom on their way to the first aid station. They all looked dazed and bleary-eyed appearing to be suffering from battle fatigue. Some were on crutches and hobbled along on one leg, others had various limbs bandaged. A few had bandages over their eyes being led along by the hand of a comrade. There was no cheering as they passed by, only an awesome comprehension of what the Canadians had to expect.

Horses and gun carriages rumbled past them, spluttering mud about, their drivers shouting for them to stop and let them pass. Calum pondered as he stopped, I wonder how many of these poor animals will be killed in this man's war!

Suddenly the sergeant ordered,

"OK reform into your sections let's march on".

They trudged over a muddy rise in the ground, the mud sticking to their boots making it increasingly difficult to lift their feet carrying a full kit.

As they came over the rise the rain ceased and the barren scene before them was of a landscape pock marked with cavernous shell holes, lines of barbed wire and a number of slit trenches. He could see puffs of smoke and hear the noise of heavy guns with shells bursting over the ground. As he looked at the trenches he was bemused by the steel helmets of their soldiers that appeared to bob up and down as they fired their rifles a machine gun opened up from an enemy position.

"OK lads let's make for the trench over there".

They arrived gasping from the effort of breaking into a run bearing their heavy kit and ended up with some of them stumbling head first into the trench. It was an empty reserve trench where its previous occupants must have left in a hurry, as there was half eaten food which had been left on plates resting on the wet ledges cut into to the sides of the earth.

"Where is the front line?" he asked the sergeant.

"200 yards ahead" was the reply.

As he said this there was a flare that lit up the sky in the fading light followed by a number of incoming shells, which exploded over their forward positions.

"Gas! Gas! Gas! Put your gas masks on!" The shout went up.

All of them desperately fumbled in their kit for gas masks as the yellowish cloud advanced. They had received training for such an event. He jerked his mask out of his bag and put it on, then replaced his helmet. One of their company must have had a faulty mask for he suddenly choked and coughed up blood. A medic attended to the poor fellow before another mask was placed over his face.

"Bastards" one them shouted beneath his mask; "They started this".

Once the musty cloud had passed they were given the all clear to remove their masks and he moved along the dugout to find a niche where he could make it his own and settle for the night.

Their company captain was looking through a periscope to see outside the trench, then satisfied, he put it down and ordered;

"Keep your heads down beneath the parapet in case of sniper fire"

Having prepared his own place, Calum made his way to the underground cooking area walking over wooden boards that had been placed on the muddy floor. They squelched as he trod over them. At the cooking area he was given hot vegetable soup in his billycan. On returning to his position, he sat on a ledge, took his coat off and covered himself with a blanket for the night but although tired, the night seemed endless as he only managed to doze for short periods, being woken by the roar of guns that was accompanied by flashes and the light of flares over their positions.

The following morning he was awake at 0700 hours and issued a mug of tea and burnt toast. The tea tasted of paraffin; he reckoned that by accident, somebody must have spilt it over the tea boxes to make it taste that way. As he sipped it and ate his toast their own guns started shelling the German lines.

At 0755 they were ordered to fix bayonets and get ready to go over the top. They were to back up the main attack. A few prayers were spoken and then at 0800 precisely their bombardment stopped. There was smoke everywhere as the Germans retaliated with a barrage of shells whizzing over and bursting behind them. He thought nervously, I only hope they don't find the range of their trench before they went over the top. He nervously clutched his Indian charm and eagle feather that Long Wolf had given to him back in Canada for protection.

"May the spirits be with me?" he murmured to himself.

Then their captain blew his whistle and ordered them out of the trench to advance towards the enemy. He watched his captain climb out only to be sliced in two as an enemy shell found its range.

"Eyes front and move out Mcdonall" shouted his sergeant as the regimental piper began playing to urge them on.

As he climbed out over the parapet, it was complete mayhem infront of him. There were shouts and cries from soldiers in battle and the crackle of rifle fire was being outdone by the noise of machine gun fire coming from the enemy lines. His adrenaline urged him on as he zigzagged over the ground, which had become a quagmire, occasionally taking cover in a shell hole. The area was littered with bodies and retreating Tommies but when they saw the Canadian advance; they turned around and joined them. Men fell alongside him as their lines were mown down. He was lucky to escape the barrage of fire when with a sigh of relief he jumped into their front trench that had now been occupied by the Germans.

He landed on his feet and had his first sight of the enemy. As he looked round the survivors of his company were now attacking its German occupants. Without hesitation, he shot a surprised German closest to him and another tried to shoot him from 5 yards but missed. With a Mcdonall war cry he cold bloodily disposed of him by thrusting his bayonet into his grey clad torso.

What have I done? The blood oozed out of the German's mouth as he muttered;

"Got in Himmel", then he slumped over.

Oh my, it could have been me! He pondered.

"Mcdonall! Don't just stand there kill the stragglers," rasped his corporal.

Now it was their turn to mow down the retreating Germans.

Once the fighting had subsided, there followed a temporary silence which was only punctuated by the sound of wailing from wounded soldiers of both sides laying on the battlefield some of them crying out for their mothers as they lay mortally wounded.

Along with others he was dispatched to check the fallen and remove the dead from the trench. This proved a gory detail, picking up those with their entrails hanging out and pieces of flesh and bone all that remained of bodies blown apart.

"Mug of tea Mcdonnall? You did well under fire" the voice of his sergeant steadied his nerves.

"Aye, I think I need one" he replied.

"You know you move like an Indian and I would like you to take a patrol out into no-mans land tonight to recover our dead and wounded".

"Aye sarg" he responded.

This proved to be the daily routine where attack, counter attack, advance, retreat, being gassed, digging in and building new defences, tunnelling towards the enemy positions resulted in ground being taken or lost during offensives of both sides.Within months he was promoted to sergeant, his own company sergeant having been killed along with 2/3 of his company. They had now advanced no more than seven miles by the time winter had set in when conditions were extremely difficult for both sides. All the time his luck held out missing bullets by a whisker and avoiding shells. The Canadians were given a brief break from the front with leave in Armetieres for a few days, where much drinking and debauchery by the troops took place.

 On their return to the front, which again had reached stalemate, he was given the duty of carrying out nightly reconnaissance patrols. On one occasion, he found a British corpse in a half flooded shell hole.

 He was sitting in the water up to his waist with his eyes fixed looking forward as if in a trance. As they moved him his helmet fell off and in the light of a shell flash they could see he was no more than a boy. Calum noticed a notebook in his pocket, he took it out and opened it and what he read considerably moved him and his companions. On the first page there were details of his next of kin who were to be notified on his death. On the second page there was a poem which read;

THE JOURNEY TO OBLIVION

Dawn is breaking

Its just before sunrise

The shelling has stopped

Men looked frightened and check their weapons

Some are praying

The officer's whistle blows

Its time to go

Lines of khaki emerge from their trenches

Most will never return

Only a few will survive

To die another day

May God rest my soul

Private Arthur Jones, 5th Battalion, Middlesex Regiment

With tears in their eyes, they looked at him; what a waste of a young life, well he certainly reached his oblivion in this foul war. Calum placed his Indian charm inside the young lad's tunic and chanted a few Indian words to take the lad's spirit into his after life. They then returned to their lines with the body, and passed his notebook to their officer to make sure it was sent back to his family in Blighty.

Then in February 1916 the inevitable happened. During one of his nightly patrols as he was cutting through barbed wire, he was shot through the stomach by a sniper and was stretchered back to the lines, then onto a field hospital. On examination, his wound was considered to be quite serious so he was sent back to England for an operation to remove the bullet.

This event turned out to be a happy interlude for him taking him away from the carnage of war torn France and Belgium. After his hospital operation he was transferred to Oldbridge House in Sussex to convalesce with other wounded soldiers. There he met a pretty young nurse with auburn hair called Janet Wilson. She was petite in build, strong in character and besides being very caring; she was witty and fascinating in conversation. Every time she talked she had a certain amount of charm about her and exuded confidence and understanding. He took an instant liking to her and their relationship developed into more than that of nurse and patient.

They became close friends and he admired her jovialality and inspiration to others making them realise they were still wanted and not forgotten. After the operation to remove the bullet, for the first few weeks he was confined to a wheelchair and as the winter turned into the spring of 1916, when she could, she took pleasure in wheeling him around the grounds of the House, particularly when she was off duty When hearing the latest news from the front he realised how lucky he was in being away from it all and being wounded.

 As she wheeled him along the pathways never before was his admiration for the colour and fragrance of the ground's flowerbeds of crocuses and daffodils came into his mind. After the traumatic experience he'd been through, he also appreciated the fermenting smell of wet woodland in the spring sunshine and the sight newly sprouted tree leaves producing a splash of fresh green against the dark timber. It was as if the trees had suddenly woken from their dark wintry slumber.

"Calum look at those wild primroses over there" she remarked as she turned the wheel chair round to give him a good view.

"Aye, I think I'm lucky to see all this compared to those poor souls over there. I'm also lucky to have you as a close friend and nurse".

"What is the name of your fiancée back in Canada?"

"Sinead; why do you ask?"

"Is she pretty?"

"Aye, I reckon she is, here's a photograph of her"

Janet looked at it, then handed it back. to him and noticed an envelope protruding from his pocket.

"My she's a lucky girl, and what's that other envelope in your pocket?"

"Oh its over a hundred year old letter that belonged to one of my ancestors, it can only be shown if I were to visit Scotland".

"Can I see it?" she asked.

"No regretfully not Janet, it is a secret that is to be kept within our family unless one of us visits Scotland.

"What would happen to it if you were to be killed in this war?"

"Then it will be sent back to my family in Canada along with the rest of my personal effects".

He replaced the photograph back inside his pocket alongside the envelope. She placed a blanket over his legs and he shivered as he said; "I feel a chill wind in the air, so we'd best be getting back to the House".

As they arrived back to the main entrance of the House, he saw what was to become a regular occurrence of men at the end of their convalescence who, back in uniform, leaving the House to return to active duty. Some looked apprehensive, he was certain that those who had been treated for shell shock should never be returned to the front but the desperation of the war situation in Europe and elsewhere demanded it. Everyone after limited recuperation was being posted back.

Over the next few months he recovered enough to help Janet with the other patients, walking round the grounds on his own and absorbing the beauty of an English summer. The pain of his wound abated with time to allow him to perform some gardening work in the grounds. He wrote numerous letters to Sinead and his family back in Canada taking time to explain his friendship with Janet.

In July it was suggested by the doctors and nursing staff to put on a pantomime as a morale booster for the patients and the local community. Janet immediately volunteered Calum to take part. He reluctantly agreed not having acted before. As it turned out, he was persuaded to take a lead part playing King Arthur in a Scottish version of "Camelot" called "Cannielot". The pantomime was to be performed on a temporary stage in the main dining hall. Janet helped him to learn his lines and tested him repeatedly.

"OK Calum the first scene is set in a fictitious kingdom in northern Britain and Merlin is on stage when you come on in your kingly robes and wearing a crown; what do you say?"

"Eh, hello Merlin my old fruit, just popped out for a spell have we! Haw haw haw!

Oh I see (seeing audience) we have some more visitors, do you think I should speak to them? (Merlin nods).What ho! (audience responds) I say I couldn't hear you, I'll say it again What ho! (audience responds louder)

That's better, its absolutely spiffing to see you. Welcome to Cannielot and to my castle, those of you in the first three rows will see the moat's dried up; I only hope my humour hasn't. Haw haw haw! Well thank you for coming, What ho Roger! (shouting to the sound man at the back of the hall) He's the lodger you know! Well I hope you'll enjoy your visit to my castle, I think I can trust you lot not like the blighters that came from Edinburgh last week. Do you what they did? They only pinched three suits of armour, Guinevere's night dress and my spare throne which they put on top of Arthur's seat in Edinburgh for a joke. What's worse they also pinched her chastity belt and put it on display with the crown jewels in Edinburgh Castle".

"That was very good a bit of ad-libbing but an excellent rendition of the script," remarked Janet.

"Then Guinnie shouts out Arthur! Arthur! And you say?"

"Coming dear, quick Merlin I've given her slip while we were out shopping, make me invisible or something"

Guinnie continues to shout, "Are there you are, where have you been, I was in Woolworth's, turned round and you were gone. "And you say?" prompted Janet.

"My, my, Guinnie dear you do look striking did you walk into a revolving door! Haw haw haw."

"That's fine Calum we'll continue after some tea" finished Janet.

Over the next few weeks the rehearsals became more intense and when it came to the first night performance he experienced a different set of nerves to that he'd had in the trenches. Everybody enjoyed the pantomime, especially the humour, costumes and scenery that had been made by the staff. It gave him a great satisfaction performing before a live audience and making people laugh again in these difficult times. The pantomime was performed over three nights and once it was over he relaxed into a false sense of security.

At the beginning of September he was declared fit by the doctors to return to active service and on September 15 he received his orders to report for duty in France by the end of the month. When Janet heard the news she reacted;

"Oh Calum my dear, I don't want you to go, I think I've fallen in love with you".

He took by the hand and looked into her eyes,

"So have I with you, you know I'm not sure if I will survive this war and ever see you or Sinead again, so lets make the most of our remaining time together" he replied.

They embraced each other and for the first time they kissed. Then she tugged away from his grip and said,

"Lets go some where tonight where we can be alone. I've got some money we can leave later and catch the train to Brighton and stay there the night. When is you have to leave?"

"The day after tomorrow" he answered.

They quickly went to the head doctor and matron and requested a pass for 24 hours. Both knew of their growing relationship and were very sympathetic to their situation granting them permission. After a train delay, they eventually arrived in Brighton on a warm autumn evening and once they'd booked in at a guesthouse as a married couple, they wandered hand in hand along the promenade enjoying the late evening sun then sat on the pebble beach. As they watched the waves roar in and break over the stones he could smell and taste the saltiness in the air; quite different he thought from the smell of rotting flesh and mud which he was use to.

The attraction for her was quite different to that he had for Sinead. It was if there was a sense of urgency about their love. My God! He thought, the number of human relationships that must be on a knife-edge due to this bloody war! They gazed into each other's eyes, they knew what they both wanted and after an evening meal they made their way back to the guesthouse.

. That night he was overwhelmed by her sexuality as they made love till the early hours of the morning. The softness of her naked body only increased his desire to make love.

The following morning commenced with a hearty English breakfast and just as they gathered their things together and about to depart she said; "Oh my darling, I forgot to tell you; yesterday before we left, I received a letter from my niece; she's paying me a visit next week. Pity you can't meet her, she has the same name as yours and comes from Scotland, a place called Glen Beag I think. She's the daughter of the estate Factor there".

He froze for a moment and didn't reply.

"Did you hear what I said"

"Aye: Glen Beag you say, are you sure?"

"Yes I'm almost certain"

"Well I don't want to hear anymore", he replied

He said nothing further about it as they travelled by train back to Olbridge House. His mind became muddled and unclear which affected his affection for her. Underneath he knew the reason why, for she had suddenly turned out to be a distant relation to the Factor of Glen Beag and the family of Murdo Mcdonall on whom his great great grandfather had placed a curse. Oh no! He thought how did he allow himself to fall in love with a distant relative of Murdo Mcdonall! Why did he not take heed of the warning when she asked to see the letter It's a good job he was reporting back tomorrow. The last thing he needed at the moment was to meet the daughter of the Factor of Glen Beag.

They spent their last evening together cuddled up infront of the House's living room fire. The warmth from its flames supplemented his dieing passion for her. They did not talk about the future; in her heart although she loved him dearly she knew his chances of survival were slim and if he did, he would return to Canada and Sinead. For his part, he knew inside there was now an obstacle to his continued love for her and what's more, he didn't rate his chances of surviving the war. It was if a happy episode in their lives was drawing to a close.

The following morning he was back in uniform and the time had come to leave Oldbridge House. He thanked and said his goodbyes to the doctors and nurses, and then before he climbed into the waiting lorry he embraced Janet and kissed her. They clung to each other, as they knew full well this could be the last time.

"Come on Sarg don't make a meal of it, its time to go" said the driver impatiently.

Their eyes lingered on each other for the last time.

"God bless you my dear Janet, I hope our spirits can sort themselves out before we meet again; take care my love".

"I'll always love you, please write to me if you can" she replied, sobbing on another nurse's shoulder.

His final glimpse of her was frantically waving to him and being constrained by staff as the lorry departed through the gates.

Within a week he was back on the front line with the Canadian Corps at a place called Neuville St. Vaast near Arras in France. and he was given the job with his section of excavating tunnels towards the German lines. These were no ordinary tunnels, they were lit by electricity and inside, and they had dressing stations, ammunition stores, operational headquarters and underground accommodation for soldiers. They were resistant to bombardment and had ventilation shafts to give them adequate air supply.

This made a change for him from the mud and filth he'd previously experienced. There was a problem however, with rats that soon found the tunnels to be more of a home for them than the trenches above.

Although he felt safer in the tunnels, the only thing he missed was besides the fresh air, sitting in a trench and admiring the ever-changing skyscape between the fighting.

He survived the winter of 1916 and due to his experience, was given the job of nightly patrols in no-mans land laying barbed wire and recovering the wounded or dead. The Germans also sent out patrols but there seemed to be some understanding between them of not firing on each other when both sides were recovering their dead.

By the spring of 1917 the allies were ready to attack from their lines around Arras. His last letter to Sinead was written from the front at the beginning of April 1917 and read;

"My dear and sweetest love,

We're getting ready for a big push; our guns have been bombarding the enemy lines for the last two

weeks...

Its now two days since we started the attack having caught Jerry by surprise and I now have time to continue this letter during the latest lull in fighting allowing me to write with some sense of sanity. Excuse me if my words falter, that means I'm interrupted by another whistle of a shell aimed at our trenches. Words yet again fail me to describe the human carnage here. Its now worse than ever and I'm at the end of my tether, we have a roll call after every attack and yesterday twenty six members of my company caught it, some of them blown up. All this for a shell scared hill called Vimy Ridge. Its only feature is burnt stumps of trees on its slopes but it is strategically significant for us to take it.

Oh I wish it could vanish and we could all go home but we have to be steadfast and see this war through in the sense of righteousness. Since my last letter I've been shot in the arm, gassed once again, had another bout of diarrhoea and my feet continue to give me agony from trench foot. Yes I'm out of the tunnels and back in the trenches!

The good news is I've finally been promoted to Lieutenant so I'm expected to lead the raid tonight. People back in Canada may laugh at all this, but its no game it's bloody serious. I hope the Generals are happy for we gained twenty-two yards yesterday and took forty-five prisoners. The bastards in the machine gun nest who'd been mowing down our men over the past few days were finally overcome and bayoneted.

There go the guns again! Is it our bombardment? Who cares! At least if my number comes up tonight I hope the spirits of the dead soldiers in the afterlife will know who won this war. Still if it is my turn, at least I know I die in good company!

The eagle has landed

See you soon

All my love

Calum"

He wrote the same letter to Janet except he signed it "Your very dear friend, Calum".

The Canadians took Vimy Ridge in mid April 1917, but Calum was wounded with shrapnel in the leg during the last push for the hill. He was also shot in the chest as he led his men up to the barbed wire. The bullet penetrated his breast pocket but his silver tobacco box containing the torn letter from 1780 deflected the bullet and saved his life. Nether less, the flesh wound and the shrapnel in his leg was sufficient to send him back to a transfer station behind the lines for treatment and he was eventually shipped back to Canada on a hospital ship.

On disembarking at the quayside in Halifax he was given a hero's welcome where he was met by Sinead, his Aunt Fiona, Archie and Long Wolf from Bhreac Farm, the latter two being the descendants of Alastair and Chaku.

Although very weak, he married Sinead at Bhreac Farm later that year, but his health gradually deteriorated with stomach and lung problems, which the doctor attributed to war wounds and him being gassed in the war. In 1919 he died from his wounds at the farm leaving Sinead a young widow. He was buried with full military honours on the farm alongside the other members of the family. The Indians chanted as he lay peacefully in his coffin and placed the eagle feather inside that he 'd carried throughout the war with beads and charms to lay his spirits to rest.

Sinead wrote to Janet at Oldbridge House to inform her of Calum's death, but the letter was returned marked "Person Unknown".

Fiona left the farm shortly afterwards to study law at Fredericton University from where she graduated in 1923. She left Canada to seek employment in the United States and her whereabouts in that country remain unknown.

Chapter 6 – Glen Beag Visit

It was the early part of August 2001 when a coach carrying American tourists pulled into the Glen Beag Hotel situated at the mouth of the glen for a two-night stop. The hotel built in 1980, had recently achieved a 4 star rating with the Tourist Board. Next to the hotel was a craft centre, which sold typical Scottish souvenirs.

As it was late afternoon, the shop was being kept open for the Americans and when they went inside it was aloud with noise from taped music by a Scottish country-dance band playing a foursome reel.

They were given an hour to spend shopping and rummaging around before they were required to return to the hotel for an evening meal. In the party were Tom De Loren and his companion Bill Watson.

Tom was unmarried, athletic for his forty-six years of age, of medium build and height with dark hair. Bill was younger, married, fair haired, slim and tall. He had come on this holiday with Tom without his wife who unfortunately, could not take the time off from her professional stage show in New York. They both worked for a large banking firm in New York and had become friends 6 year's ago.

Both were interested in Scottish history particularly that of clans in the highlands. They looked at the various assortments of tweed jackets, golf sweaters, Arran jumpers, tartan ties, kilts and skirts, deerstalker hats, plastic handled dirks and skean dubhs. The kilts they noted from the labels were factory produced. Besides the mass produced Loch Ness monster teddies and dolls, ceramic figures of highlanders; some playing bagpipes, and cheap models of wild animals and highland cattle, there was nothing on sale that related to the history of the area.

Tom looked at the assortment of kilts on the rack. "Is this one the Mcdonall tartan?" he asked the woman shop assistant.

"I think it is" was the reply as she searched for the label. "Aye it is" after she read it. "It's a very good quality kilt made in the Borders".

He then looked at the ties and found a Mcdonall one but it was in a different tartan. "Why is this different?" he asked.

"Ooch aye it's the dress tartan of the clan which is worn nowadays at special events".

"Was this not the clan that inhabited Glen Beag ?" he asked her. "How did you know that aye it was, you seem to be very knowledgeable", she replied.

Bill was also fascinated by Tom's knowledge. Tom bought a Mcdonall tie for Bill as a present and they both returned to the hotel for drinks before the evening meal.

As part of the package tour, tomorrow would be a shooting and fishing trip in the glen. They would have to breakfast early to make the most of a full day.

The evening meal in the dining room consisted of Scotch broth, fresh grilled trout, and potatoes with fresh vegetables, followed by a choice of sweets or cheese and biscuits. They consumed the meal with glasses of French wine bought by Bill. It was well cooked and appetising. They finished the meal with two cups of ground coffee.

They retired to the bar after the meal mingling with the other tourists and ordering two malt whiskies. The bar was modern but the walls and furniture were designed to look like a 1930's imitation décor, which was ill fitting and didn't blend in.

There was a smell of stale cigar smoke. Suddenly the outside door opened and a stocky man with red cheeks quickly strode into the bar. He looked wet and dishevelled, probably from the rain, which had started an hour ago. He was middle aged, dressed in a check shirt that half hung out of his mud splattered overalls. He was a typical rustic man wearing farmer's boots.

"Who is that?" Tom asked the barman.

"Oh that's Angus he's the forester from the Glen Beag Estate. He comes in here twice a week for a drink and blether" was the reply.

Tom caught Angus's eye and advanced towards him. "Can I buy you a drink?" he asked.

"Aye but if it's a lift you want up to the big hoose I dinna have any room in my Land rover except for a wee one".

He introduced Bill. "We are staying here for the next two nights, would you like to join us at our table.?"

"Aye, but I canna stay for too lang" was the reply.

There was a clatter and humdrum in the bar with the various conversations going on so Tom found a table in the corner where they could hear themselves speak. They told him they were on holiday but both had a special interest in highland history. They asked various questions about Glen Beag and its history.

Angus told them that the estate belonged to private consortium and he'd been a forester on it for sixteen years. The consortium arranged grouse and deer shooting holidays for corporate companies and their top executives and Glen Beag House which was originally built as a tower house and later extended with fortified turrets, was now classified as a hydro centre providing leisure and sporting facilities. The grounds also had a golf course.

"Was this big house not formally named Ardonall House which was the seat of the Chief of the Clan Mcdonall?" asked Tom.

"Aye it was" Angus replied.

"How did the house come under new ownership?" he asked. Bill remained very attentive and surprised at Tom's questions.

"Ooch I think it was in the late 18th century when the 6th Chief squandered and gambled his fortune away in London gaming houses. The story told to me by the gillie on the estate was that the House was put up as a wager which he lost".

"And what of the clans people who lived in the glen?" asked Tom again.

"Murdo Mcdonall the Factor reckons they were all evicted under the Hieland clearances" was the reply.

Bill topped up their whisky glasses.

"Aye it must have been very sad for the people;" retorted Bill.

" Murdo has worked on the estate for thirty years and he reckons the glen is haunted by the spirits of the people that lived here a long time ago. He said during twilight hours he has even heard a woman and children screaming at the far end of the glen and felt that something tragic must have happened up there", related Angus.

" Violent times compared to the peace of this area today" said Bill.

Tom remained silent but attentive. Suddenly he spoke,

"Were there not Tacksmen working for the Chief during the evictions?"

"I dinna ken Tacksmen, you'd best be asking Murdo about that you'll see him in the morn as he will be your instructor on the shooting trip. The hotel has a contract with the estate to arrange their shooting and fishing trips," replied Angus.

They then compared the various lifestyles between Scotland and America. Their conversation ended when Angus looked at his watch. "I'd be away noo fore the police pay their usual visit; with all this whisky I've drunk I canna afford to be breathalysed, I thank you for your blether and hope tomorrow's shooting and fishing goes well". Angus speedily left the bar as he did when he came in.

They drank one more glass of whisky before deciding to retire to their rooms for the night. It was going to be an early start and a busy day tomorrow.

Before Bill fell asleep he pondered over the information that they obtained from Angus. If his wife were here she would say the story of the haunted glen would make a good play and set to music; a stage show like Brigadoon. He thought Tom had been a bit relentless in his questioning and this was not typical of the Tom De Loren he knew.

Bill was wakened by an early morning call from the hotel receptionist. He looked at his watch it showed 6.45am. Breakfast for those going on the shooting and fishing trip was 7.15am.

He quickly showered and shaved, putting on warm clothing and his walking boots to prepare for the trip. He then went to Tom's room and knocked on the door. There was no answer.

He decided to go downstairs to see if Tom was already at breakfast. Sure enough, there was Tom on his own sitting at a table in the corner of the dinning room tucking into a plate of porridge.

"Morning Tom, looks like a fine morning" he said.

"Morning" replied Tom.

They talked about the day's shooting and fishing trip, which they both looked forward to. It appeared to Bill, as he plunged his spoon into a plate of corn flakes that Tom seemed rather distant and preoccupied as they talked.

They ate a full cooked British breakfast and finished it with black coffee. Tom was also appropriately dressed for their outdoor activity and they returned to their rooms to pick up their waterproofs.

They came downstairs to join the other guests who were taking the trip. There were about twelve of them, all men; their wives having booked alternative transport for a shopping trip to Inverness.

They climbed into one of the two people carriers provided by the hotel that would be transporting them up the glen. The time was 7.40am and for August the weather was exceptionally mild. The forecast for the day was sunny with light westerly winds and showers. Their driver said that the estate's gillie and his beaters would meet them for the grouse shooting at the far end of the glen.

As they started off they drove past a few cottages with typical English names, some of them the driver said, were only used as weekend cottages. He reckoned they had been built a few years after the hotel was established. It seemed strange to them that names like "Westfield" and "Rose" were given to cottages in a highland glen. By the appearance of their gardens and what they could see of the cars parked outside their garages it was evident that no crofters were living in them.

As they drove on, the terrain became more rugged and the tarmac road very narrow with passing places. They passed a group of hippies encamped in the ruins of what must have been an original settlement in the glen. They could not avoid noticing them with the loud and deafening noise of heavy metal music issuing forth from their ghetto blasters. They had also appeared to have desecrated the ruined walls with paint daubs of "Down with Tony Blair".

Bill cast a glance at Tom and noticed his lips were trembling with rage. "How could they!" he murmured.

The people carriers were driven further up into the glen and a brief stop made for a picture shoot of the scenery that was now glowing from the early morning sunrays. Many of the men got out of the vehicles and started taking photographs including Bill but Tom remained in his seat preoccupied with something he took out of his pocket.

"I'll take some photographs for you" Bill shouted to Tom through the car window. Tom nodded in agreement.

Five minutes later they were on their way again. The driver told them that the tallest mountain on the right was Ben Breac. They did not meet any vehicles on the road until they arrived at their destination. It was 8.30am.

Three Land rovers and a minibus were already parked in a rough stone area where the road came to an abrupt end. There were some thirty men standing around awaiting their arrival. They got out of their people carrier along with the other members of the party.

One man strode forward and introduced himself. He was middle aged, rather dapper, dressed in tweeds and plus fours, and a deerstalker hat. "Morning, my name is Murdo Mcdonall, I'm the Factor from the Glen Beag Estate and these are my ghillies and grouse beaters for today. Those of you that have not used sporting guns before will be given tuition. My gundogs will retrieve the shot grouse for you and those who can bag the most will have them for their evening meal back at the hotel. I'll also be around to guide you to the loch and show you the best fishing places this afternoon. The loch is about two miles away and you will have to travel on foot to reach it. Any questions?"

"How far is it to the grouse shooting? As I cannot walk that distance to the loch for I suffer from gout in my foot" asked a member of the party. "About two hundred yards as the beaters will drive the grouse to where you'll be in the gun line. As regards fishing this afternoon, the hotel should have warned you that there was a two-mile walk to the loch. Those who do not wish to take the fishing trip will be returned to the hotel, as you will not be allowed to wander off on private property" he replied.

Bill thought his manner was rather offhand.

For the next hour those who couldn't shoot were given tuition while the beaters made off through the heather to circle round and drive the grouse back towards them as they formed a shooting line some two hundred yards from the parking area.

They were issued guns and were asked if they knew how to use them. They both explained they had used similar guns on sporting trips in the States.

The gundogs, which had been in the back of the Land rovers, were brought out and reigned in along the line of guns.

Suddenly there was crescendo of fire as the guns blasted at the fleeing grouse disturbed by the beaters. They bagged a couple each which were retrieved by two of the dogs nearby.

They were then told to alter the gun line to the other side of the road and the whole process was repeated with the grouse being driven towards them from another direction. They managed to bag another three grouse with their guns.

"OK let's take a break for coffee" said Murdo looking at his watch.

They all returned to the parking area and gathered round the parked vehicles where the drivers produced sandwiches and flasks of coffee from the boot. The fresh air had made them thirsty and hungry so they drank and consumed the sandwiches offered by the drivers without any persuasion. Suddenly Murdo approached and spoke to them,

"I've been watching you both, so you two reckon you are good shots, well I've probably shot more grouse than you've had hot dinners, see here, showing his sporting rifle, I can kill a stag with this from two hundred and fifty yards!"

"Good for you" said Bill thinking what a braggart he is.

"I understand your surname is Mcdonall" intervened Tom.

"Was your family from this glen?"

Murdo looked at him with disdain,

"That's correct, " he said proudly.

"My family has lived in this glen for four hundred years, my ancestors were Chief Tacksmen to the Clan Chief until misfortune fell upon them and the Chief in the late 18th century. My job is now Factor to the estate

"What type of misfortune?" asked Tom.

" I'm not prepared to talk about it" he replied.

"Certainly not to foreigner's. OK let's shoot some more grouse, you lot get out there and do some more beating!" he shouted at the grouse beaters as he walked away from them in a swagger.

"What do you think of him?" Bill asked Tom.

"Bullish, self opinionated, rude and dangerous" answered Tom.

"What is a Tacksman?" asked Bill.

" A person that managed the tenants of the land for the Clan Chief, nowadays he would known as the estate Factor; do you want to do some more grouse shooting?"

"No let's walk down to the loch," answered Bill. They then handed in their guns before setting off.

 They walked along the two-mile track to the loch. The sun was still shining and there was warmth in the air emanating from the peaty muir. They reached the loch after sauntering along the track for thirty minutes.

 There they met a man from the estate who introduced himself as another gillie called John, who explained he was in charge of the fishing gear kept in a hut.

"I'll just issue these rods and tackle to you that includes all the flies you'll need to catch trout in this loch. I take it you are with the party from the hotel?"

"Yes" they said. He looked hard at Tom as if he was trying to remember if he had seen his face before.

"Don't I know you from somewhere?" he asked.

"I hardly think so, I'm from New York" answered Tom.

"I'm sure I know your face from somewhere, Oh well this is your fishing gear I hope you can catch some. The best place is on the west side of the loch in the shade, I'll tell Murdo that you're here". He then took his mobile phone out of his pocket to ring his Factor.

They both picked up their gear and walked off along the banks. The loch was now sparkling in the midday sun. Tom glanced back a few times and saw the John talking on the telephone and pointing in their direction.

They found a sheltered spot on the bank and decided to eat their packed lunch before fishing. They had been there some twenty-five minutes when they saw a dirty Land rover bumping its way towards them.

"I thought they said the loch was inaccessible for vehicles!" exclaimed Bill.

As the Land rover drew nearer and they could see an enraged Murdo inside desperately trying to control the vehicle. It drew up alongside them and Murdo flew out tripping over himself on the way.

"You Yankee bastards, I didn't give you permission to break off from the shooting party! You can have two hours fishing, and then you must return your gear to the fish keeper and walk back to the transport. Is that clearly understood?"

"How dare you talk to your clients this way, I will be reporting you to the Glean Beag management on our return" said Bill.

"Do as you like but I'm the authority here; and what do you have you say; do you have a tongue in your head?" He then turned and challenged Tom.

Tom eyeballed him and calmly replied,

"Do know anything about this?" He took out of his pocket an envelope and from it a faded piece of paper with writing on it, which looked like a letter that had been torn to pieces and stuck back together. He passed it to Murdo who became graven and white faced as he read it.

Trembling Murdo became stuck for words; his self-confidence had disappeared in an instant.

"Eh! Eh where did you get this from?" he stuttered.

"It was given to me by a friend who knew I was coming to Scotland" said Tom.

"Oh no its not possible, it can't be possible!" mumbled Murdo taking a good long look at Tom. Shaking, he had difficulty in standing and handing the letter back; he did so avoiding Tom's piercing eyes. He then turned about and still shaking climbed back into his Land rover. He started it up, revved the engine and sheepishly drove away.

"What was that all about?" asked Bill "You certainly gave him a fright".

Tom placed the paper back inside the envelope then returned it to his pocket.

"You'll find out in due course" he replied.

They fly fished for the next three hours along with other members of their party, which by now had joined them from the grouse shooting. Although he only allowed them two hours for fishing, Murdo did not appear again at the loch. Although there was the occasional bite, they couldn't catch any fish.

It was now 4.00pm and the sun's rays seem to make the loch water clearer, midges were now becoming a problem so they decided to make their way back. They returned their gear back to the hut of John the fish keeper. They followed behind the other members their party who also decided to call it a day. Half way along the track between the loch and the parking area Tom suddenly stopped.

" I seem to have lost my signet ring, it must be back at the fishing spot; I'm going back for it; you carry on and I'll meet you back at the car park" he said.

"Can you find your way back?" asked Bill.

" Oh yes, don't worry I can keep in contact through my mobile phone" he replied.

Bill kept on following the other party members, the last he saw of Tom was disappearing over a rocky outcrop some distance away. Bill reached the parking area and mingled with the other Americans exchanging stories over the events of the day.

It was 5.00pm when the minibus left full of beaters along with two of the Land rovers carrying the ghillies loaded with the guns and dogs. The two people carriers and the remaining Land rover held on for the return of Tom. There was no sign of Murdo anywhere. They tried to contact him by mobile phone and Bill likewise with Tom. There was no reply from either of them. Evidently, Murdo had returned to the parking area in one of the Land rovers just after 1.15pm and then wandered off. They thought he was off to check out the whereabouts of the glen's deer herd so he knew where to take tomorrow's shooting party from Glen Beag House. Or they reckoned he could have walked across country back to his house on the estate.

John now turned up having finished for the day.

"Have you passed my friend as you came along the track?" Bill asked him. "He's gone back to search for his signet ring which he says he must have dropped where we were fishing".

"No, he didn't pass me along the track" was the reply.

They waited another thirty minutes; by that time it was going to prove rather late for evening dinner by the time the party got back to the hotel.

"I'll go back and search for Mr De Loren; you take the rest of the party back to the hotel" John told the drivers of the two people carriers.

"I'll stay with you," said Bill showing concern for his friend.

"OK, you can help me search for him" was the reply.

Within a few minutes the American party alighted the people carriers and they set off back down the glen. The remaining Land rover was left for the use of the John and for taking Tom and Bill back to the hotel.

As they walked back up the track to the loch the sun became hazy and the evening mist was starting to form in the glen. It took them 45 minutes to reach the place where they'd been fishing however; there was no sign of Tom. They searched the banks of the loch and scanned the braes of the glen; again, there was no sign of him. By now the weather was changing and in the mist that was now starting to thicken, it was beginning to drizzle with rain.

"There's no trace of him," commented John, "And the weather is closing in".

Bill tried contacting Tom again on his mobile phone; there was no answer. He remembered that Tom said he would keep in contact. They shouted his name out which echoed off the glen braes; again there was no reply.

"We had best be getting back, as its no use looking for him in these conditions; the light will be failing soon, if he's not around here, he may be sheltering in one of the shepherd's huts which are located a long way further up the glen. In these conditions, its no use calling out the rescue helicopter or the mountain rescue team as by the time they arrive it will be dark and they will have difficulty operating in this poor visibility. Our best bet if he has not turned up by the morning, is to arrange for a major search to be mounted. I will warn the authorities in the meantime."

Bill reluctantly agreed as they walked back along the track from the loch in the drizzle and thick mist. They returned to the hotel in the Land rover to find an overriding concern in the buzz of numerous conversations going on, not only over Tom's disappearance but also on Murdo, who his wife had reported missing to Glen Beag House. By now the drizzle had turned into a downpour and the Police who'd been called in, said they thought it would best to delay a search until morning.

Bill gave them Tom's mobile number so they could keep on trying to contact him. By now he was very hungry and he and John were invited to sit down to a late evening meal.

After the meal, John said he had better be getting back to his accommodation on the estate so he could have some rest before the search tomorrow He seemed to think he was responsible for not keeping an eye on them. Likewise, Bill retired to his room after holding a further conversation with the other guests.

He undressed and lay on his bed, it was now 11.00pm, he was unable to sleep with the preoccupation of his friend's disappearance on his mind. He tried once more to contact Tom by mobile telephone, but to no avail. Suddenly, there was a knock on the door! It must be Tom he thought; he must have returned. He leapt out of bed and opened the door; only to find the hotel manager asking him if he was all right and did he need a sedative to make him sleep. He declined the offer but thanked the manager for his consideration.

He fell into a sporadic slumber with snatches of sleep throughout the night keeping an ear open for a telephone call from Tom. He was up as soon as the dawn broke; dressed and went downstairs where there was already a hub of activity taking place as the search was being organised. The police were present along with the mountain rescue team with their climbing gear and the estate workers that acted as grouse beaters yesterday. All were being issued with two- way radios.

A number of the American guests had also volunteered their services and were willing to delay their tour to take part in the search. They were being briefed and he noticed Angus and John were there; both looked rather agitated and tired. A uniformed police sergeant spoke. He was a gaunt person of middle age.

"My name is Sergeant Macdonald; now that you are all here, I can tell you what the present situation is. Murdo Mcdonall and the American, Mr De Loren are both still missing, the search and rescue helicopter is due to arrive from Lossiemouth at 9.00am. We will rendezvous in the parking area at the end of the glen road and meet it there. We will split up into groups and conduct the search from there, any questions?"

"If the search takes a long time, what about food and drink?" asked one of the Americans.

"You'll be issued a packed lunch with a drink at the rendezvous point" the sergeant replied. "Now lets check our watches, I make it exactly 6.30am".

There was a general murmur of agreement. Sergeant MacDonald continued;

"The weather forecast is cloudy but dry following last night's downpour, visibility in the glen should improve by the time the helicopter arrives".

Bill quickly gulped down a cup of coffee and two slices of buttered toast before getting into a Land rover with John and Angus. They then drove up the glen past the cottages and past the hippie encampment where there was no sign of life at this time in the morning, only a smouldering of last nights camp fire which had been dampened down by the rain.

The mist was still thick enough to prevent good visibility in the glen as they arrived at the parking area in a convoy of vehicles to join the increasing gathering of searchers. The mountain rescue team were sorting out their gear and a number of the police and estate workers were busily putting on waterproof clothing.

They had been there fifteen minutes when a roar of a Harley Davidson motorcycle was heard approaching up the road. When it came into view they could see the rider was one the hippies from the encampment. It skidded as it came to a halt and the rider impatiently put it on its stand before striding across to speak to Sergeant MacDonald.

"Are you in charge?" he asked. The sergeant nodded.

He nervously spoke as the rest of the searchers gathered round.

"I understand you are about to mount a search for two missing people. Well I don't know if this is relevant, but late last evening before the mist came down and it started to rain, I was climbing up at the far end of the glen when I looked up and saw a kilted highlander standing high in amongst the rocks brandishing a sword and shield and looking down arguing with another man. Suddenly there was a cold rush of breeze and an icy feeling that made my hair stiffen in the back of my neck and the man below dressed in tweeds and wearing a deerstalker hat fell off a rocky precipice that he'd been standing on. He must have fallen about 200 feet. I was so scared that I froze and could not move for a few minutes and when I glanced up, the highlander had disappeared, so I hastily retraced my steps back down the slopes. I was so petrified I dared not look back until I reached here."

"Can you take us to where this happened?" asked the sergeant.

"I think so" he replied nervously.

He turned to the mountain rescue team.

"Ok your team can follow this lead accompanied by, what is your name?" he asked the hippie.

"Danny" was the reply.

"Ok with Danny".

Within minutes the mountain rescue team set off with Danny.

Bill listened attentively to the story but was preoccupied with Tom's safety and becoming impatient. He was allocated as Tom's friend to accompany Angus and John and another estate worker called Jamie who was a qualified first aider.

They then set off heading towards the loch. They had been walking for twenty minutes when they heard the sound of the search and rescue helicopter landing on the parking area. The mist had now cleared and there was good visibility for a change.

They searched the whole of the loch side looking for signs of human activity.

"Ooch I ken, lets away to further up the glen to the remoter part where there's a ruined croft and search around there," said Angus.

It took them another forty minutes before they reached the ruins. As they came into view they could see a human figure lying on the ground next to what appeared to be some stone cairns. They quickened their pace as they approached. As they came closer they could see the figure was a man that was motionless, dressed in a faded shirt and kilt with a broadsword and targe neatly laid out alongside.

"Oh my god its Tom; is he alive? exclaimed Bill.

" I'm afraid not" Jamie replied after examining the body. "Strange there's no injury or marks on the body; this is one for a post mortem to decide on the cause of death".

They comforted him after radioing for the helicopter to come and recover the body.

He sadly looked around; Tom was lying next to three stone cairns that appeared to mark graves. The croft was in ruins and on inside examination it looked as though it could have been destroyed by fire a long time ago. He wondered as to why Tom was dressed in a kilt with a sword and targe lying alongside him; was there some connection to the kilted highlander in the hippie's story he asked himself. He noted he was wearing his signet ring.

 Within ten minutes the helicopter turned up and Sergeant MacDonald got out and reported.

"Well, this is the second body we've found, Murdo's body was recovered an hour ago from a rocky ravine where Danny said it was. His neck and spine was broken and by the look on his face he appeared to have been really scared by something."

The sergeant searched the Tom's body and in the sporran found the envelope with the faded letter that had been torn and repaired.

"This is very old do you know anything about this?" he asked Bill.

"No but he showed it to Murdo yesterday" he replied.

 "This is very suspicious, I'll hold onto it, perhaps someone can shed some light on these very mysterious deaths" said the sergeant.

 The search was called off and the two bodies were air lifted to Inverness for a post mortem examination. The police also retrieved the sword and targe.

 On his return to the hotel he went with the manager and police to Tom's room to go through his belongings. He knew he had a duty to notify his death to his relatives, but Tom had kept himself to himself and never spoke about his family. The only person mentioned in an old letter found amongst his belongings was his mother Fiona De Loren with a New Jersey telephone number.

He rang the number in front of the police only to find that Mrs De Loren had been dead for the past six years. The police said they would try and trace Tom's other relatives and asked him if he could stay on in Scotland for another few days while they completed their investigations. He agreed to this. as he was not due to return to work until the following week.

He said a sorrowful goodbye to the other American tourists who resumed their tour after lunch in the hotel. After lunching with them he felt sleepy and decided to retire to his room, exhausted by the events over the past two days. Before lying down on his bed he thought he'd better check his mobile phone for any text messages from his wife. There were none but a message he'd missed read;

"BILL-TOM THANKS YOU FOR YOUR FRIENDSHIP-I'M AT PEACE NOW WITH SIOBHAN AND THE BAIRNS-CALUM MCDONALL".

Chapter 7 – Spirits of the Glen

He could not understand this message from somebody called Calum and after his sleep he went downstairs to see if the police were still in the hotel. He caught Sergeant MacDonald as he was about to leave and showed him the text message.

"I don't understand it either, what was the time of the message?" the sergeant asked.

"Eh, it was just before 1.00am in the early hours of this morning. he answered.

"Look I'll make a note of it and pass it on to CID. I'll go over now to see Mrs Mcdonall and interview her about her husband's death, I expect the minister is already there comforting her. I'll see you tomorrow".

After evening dinner in the hotel, He retired to the bar and reflected on the events of the past two days. Except for three other guests the bar was empty. He ordered a whisky and had been sitting there for ½ hour watching a BBC Scotland News report of the deaths of Tom and Murdo on the bar's TV, when Angus came flying through the door and made straight over to him.

"Can I join you for a blether?" he asked

"Yes of course you can" he replied, "Barman, pour a whisky for Angus".

They talked about the consequences of the death of Tom which led to him finally showing him the text message he'd received.

"Calum Mcdonall, I ken that name from somewhere, ooch aye I remember noo, a story told to me when I was a bairn aboot a Calum Mcdonall that lived in the glen during the 18th century. He murdered two of the Chief's men and was hunted down but never caught. That's the only Calum I ken but he wouldn't have had a mobile phone back in the 18th century," said Angus with a laugh.

A roar of motorcycles passing the hotel and heading out of the glen interrupted their conversation. They were the hippies that had been camped in the old ruined settlement. They both wondered if they were leaving because of being frightened after hearing Danny's story.

"You'll be away with the police to Inverness in the morn?" asked Angus.

"Yes I hope to find out more before I return to the States and make the arrangements for Tom's funeral" he replied.

Angus belched as he finished his dram of whisky.

"I'll be away noo, aye its been guid blethering with you, I'm sorry that you lost your friend and guid nicht to you. If I dinna see you again afore you travel back to the States, I wish you guid luck".

"Good night and I thank you for all your help" retorted Bill.

Angus quickly strode across the bar floor and slammed the door as he departed. A few minutes later Bill heard his noisy diesel engine start up and there was a screech of tyres as Angus's Land Rover sped off.

After another restless night spent mulling over the tragedies, the following morning, he breakfasted alone before Sergeant MacDonald arrived accompanied by another constable.

He sent the constable to Tom's room to gather his belongings for examination so they could be taken with Bill to Inverness. It took them two hours to reach Inverness travelling along a main road winding through attractive mountain scenery. The weather was dry and sunny. On arrival at Inverness Police Station, he was ushered into an interview room. He was brought a cup of tea and biscuits and was asked to wait for the Detective Inspector who wanted to interview him. He sat down readily drinking the tea provided and munching his way through the biscuits. He'd been there for what seemed twenty minutes before the door opened and a burly man with a waspish face entered, wearing plain clothes accompanied by Sergeant MacDonald. He spoke in a gruff voice. "Mr Watson, let me introduce myself, I'm Detective Inspector Malcolm, I understand you were holidaying with Mr De Loren when all this happened; please accept my condolences on the loss of your friend. Now, please tell me your side of the story."

Bill related what had happened over the past two days. He had the full attention of the inspector and sergeant who were copiously taking notes. "This is a strange case, evidently from the post mortem, Mr De Loren died from natural causes as compared to Murdo Mcdonall who died from a broken neck caused by his fall. Sergeant MacDonald told me of the text message you received on your mobile phone, which led me to doing some research. I've found out from 18th century parish records held at the museum, that there was a tenant crofter by the name of Calum Mcdonall living in the upper part of Glen Beag at that time with his wife Sioban and two children. He lost his croft, which was burnt down with his wife and children inside during the highland clearances of

Glen Beag in 1780. The faded letter found on Mr De Loren which had been torn up and stuck back together is, according to the museum, dated September 14, 1780 and a reply to a notice of eviction which was served on the family. At the bottom is the writing of Siobhan Mcdonall declaring their loyalty to the clan chief and offering a higher rent to remain at the croft. The letter has the mark of Calum Mcdonall who obviously couldn't write.

The place where Mr De Loren's body was found was at the ruins of that croft alongside the graves of probably Calum's family; all very strange if you ask me."

"I've got something to add to that" Sergeant McDonald interrupted.

"Well you know I went to see Murdo's wife yesterday, she said except in broad daylight, he very rarely went up to the upper part of the glen because he reckoned it to be haunted. She said he always told people that he was very proud of his ancestors having been hereditary Chief Tacksmen to the clan chief and living in the glen for the past four hundred years". Since the late 18th century though, the family had suffered the bad luck of a number of stillbirths, accidents and premature deaths. He himself was not feeling well over the past few days and had made a doctor's appointment for the end of the week".

"Yes, he bragged to Tom and me about his family being Chief Tacksmen to the clan chief" exclaimed Bill.

The inspector looked at a copy of the original eviction notice he'd obtained from the museum.

"Well would you believe it, do you know who signed this 1780 notice of eviction that was served on Mcdonall clansmen at that time? It was not signed by the clan chief but by the Chief Tacksman who was Murdo Mcdonall".

"Well I never, what a coincidence!" commented Sergeant MacDonald.

Bill then told them of Angus's story about Calum being an outlaw. With this information, the Detective Inspector rang up the curator of the museum who he said was an expert on clan history and folklore.

"Do you know anything about murders that was committed by Calum Mcdonall in Glen Beag in 1780?" he asked.

He listened to the reply with interest. "I see, the whole family, and he was never caught and there were rumours of a curse. Thank you very much for the information, you've been most helpful." He put the phone down.

"Well gentlemen, that again was very interesting. According to the story that's been handed down, Calum Mcdonall was not present at the time of the eviction when his croft was burnt down and his family perished inside. It was acknowledged that Murdo Mcdonall and his men carried out the burning. As revenge, Calum killed two of Murdo's men and was hunted down by redcoat soldiers but never found. He just vanished off the face of the earth, but according to highland folklore, before doing so, he placed a curse on Murdo's family."

"So the curse still exists today if you can believe what happened to Murdo." Bill commented.

"In my experience, I know of many strange occurrences and beliefs that have been reported to have happened in the glens," said Sergeant MacDonald.

"But how does the death of my American friend and the way he was dressed lying beside the croft graves have any connection to all of this?" he asked.

The sergeant continued;

"That remains a mystery for the moment, but there could be some spiritual explanation if you can believe Gaelic superstition. If there's a DNA make up from our parents inside us, why not a spiritual one that is passed on. When there is a wrongful injustice caused by violent happenings such as a murder in a family, the spirits cannot rest until there is a form of retribution, which can be associated with a curse. For spiritual retribution of wrongdoings time can be infinite, unless, in the case of Murdo and Calum Mcdonall an ancestor appears on the scene of the same bloodline into which the disturbed spirit can enter the body. Calum obviously placed a curse on Murdo and his family from which they've been suffering since the 18th century. Yesterday was the final showdown of these spirits that resulted in their deaths. I say this going by the text message you received from Mr De Loren's mobile phone sent to you by Calum.

That's why many of the glens are reputed to be haunted by spirits of highland people who suffered greatly during the time of the clearances. Those who perished during the upheaval of forced emigration are said to have left their spirits behind in their homeland. For some reason Calum's spirit must have been inside Mr De Loren and led him to a hiding place where he recovered his 18th century attire and weapons, and where he put them on to seek revenge for his family's deaths and confront Murdo's spirit inside the 21st century Murdo.

You can imagine the shock of Murdo's spirit seeing Calum again in highland dress with his weapons. No wonder he fell off a rock with fright to his death. It also explains Murdo's reaction to Mr De Loren when he showed him the original letter that was torn in pieces and stuck back together."

"I'm not aware Tom had any Scottish ancestors," said Bill.

The telephone rang again and Detective Inspector Malcolm picked it up. He put his hand over the mouthpiece and softly said to them,

"Its from America."

He removed his hand and spoke down the phone.

"Yes the name of the deceased is Tom De Loren, yes that's his address in New York; so you've found out his mother and father are dead, I see, and there are no surviving relatives. Hum, where did his parents come from? His father's family originated from Holland and his mother? From Canada then she settled in New Jersey: what was her maiden name? What was that again could you repeat it; FIONA McDONALL!"

It was raining in New York on the day of Tom's funeral when Bill and his wife with a few colleagues from the Bank stood shivering in the cold during late August.

As his friend's coffin was lowered into the grave he felt a hand on his shoulder and a tingle in his neck. He looked round and saw no one. The minister had finished giving the last rights. Only the hired piper playing a Mcdonall lament broke the silence.

Bill knew he'd have to take his wife back to Scotland next year and show her Glen Beag and Calum's ruined croft where he would place fresh heather on the graves of his family. He was also pleased that Siobhan's torn letter and a copy of the original eviction notice obtained from the museum along with Calum's plaid and weapons, had been donated to Glen Beag House where they were to be put on display with details of his story. There were also plans to erect a Celtic cross on the brae above the ruined croft in memory of what had happened there.

Since coming back from Scotland, he had attempted to trace back Tom's family on his mother's side and he had found a connection with a family that were emigrants to Nova Scotia in Canada.

Next month he was going to follow up this connection by travelling to a place called Strathloch in Nova Scotia and look at the parish records there. Sadly, this was not to happen as Bill was among those that died the following month on September 11th in the terrorist attack on the twin towers of the World Trade Centre, New York where he'd gone to have a meeting for his bank. One can only wonder what spirit of justice there will be for him and the others that innocently died in that tragedy.

However, after her bereavement for Bill, his wife travelled to Scotland the following year and witnessed the Celtic cross being erected on the brae above the ruined croft in Glen Beag. On behalf of her husband, she also paid homage to Calum's murdered family by planting heather on their graves. On the death of Tom De Loren the curse on Murdo's family was removed.

As she stood there amongst the small crowd on the day the cross was being unveiled by Conner Mcdonall, nephew of Murdo Mcdonall and

Chairman of the local Community Council, there was a warm glow as if of forgiveness in the glen and she noticed in the sunshine that separate from the crowd, there was an elderly man leaning on his stick and holding the hand of a small boy seemingly intent on watching the proceedings. After the ceremony, she also observed them walk up to the cross where the old man paused for a minute and bowed his head. Then they made their way to the graves near the ruined croft and the boy laid wreaths of heather on them.

Her curiosity overcame her inhibitions and she approached them to ask, "Do you have any connection with the family?"

The old man replied saying he was Calum Mcdonall, the love child of Janet Wilson who was a nurse in the First World war and a wounded Canadian soldier she treated called Calum Mcdonall. She named him after his father although she never told the soldier he'd fathered a love child.

He himself had only found out that he'd a family connection with Glen Beag after doing research from what his mother had told him. He also knew that his father came from Nova Scotia in Canada, but he was unable to establish the whereabouts as his mother gave him no information as to where his father had lived in the province.

"And who is this?" she asked referring to the young boy.

"This is Cailean my grandson, say hello to the American lady!"

She told him of what had happened in the glen the year before involving her late husband and the death of Tom De Loren.

"It's a good job I didn't pay a visit to the glen a year earlier then!" he remarked.

She wondered what he meant by that.

They exchanged addresses and she informed him of the possible family connection he had with a place called Strathloch in Nova Scotia where perhaps this was where his father came from. She bade them farewell and departed. The last time she saw them was walking together holding hands through the mist that had now descended upon the glen fading out the sun.When she returned to the hotel she asked other people who'd been at the ceremony if they had noticed the old man and the young boy, but they hadn't seen them.

To this day, Bhreac Farm has changed little, it is still profitable as a farm, except two miles away there is now a modern freeway to take traffic between Halifax and Truro. The descendants of Alastair and the Indians still keep a shared ownership of the farm.

The bear claw still has pride and place over the fireplace and although the wolves and eagles have long since disappeared from the forest, as you walk amongst the trees and hear the pine needles rustle overhead, you sense there is someone there. Is it the spirit of Chaku out hunting? Only you will know.

EXPLANATION OF TERMS

Glean Bheag is old gaelic for Glen Beag and translated means small glen.

Beinn Bhreac is old gaelic for Ben Breac which is the highest mountain in Glen Beag

1745 Jacobite Rebellion – The rising of highland clans which supported the Stewart kings led by Bonnie Prince Charlie the young pretender.

Culloden, near Inverness – Place of the final defeat of the Jacobite army in 1746.

Bairns – Children.

Tacksman – A person that managed the tenants of the land and collected the rent on behalf of the clan chief. Nowadays he would be called an estate Factor or Manager.

Ghillie – Person employed by the estate to look after the supply of grouse, manage the deer herds and general wildlife.

Targe – A Highlander's round shield made out of hide and wood. Used as protection in battle.

Ship's Yard – A large wooden or metal spar crossing the masts of a ship horizontally or diagonally, from which the sail is set.

League – Measurement of distance at sea of three nautical miles

Ship's Figurehead - ornamental carved and painted figure erected on the bow of the ship as a decorative or religious emblem generally expressing some aspect of the ship's name or function.

Bowsprit – a large spar projecting over the bow to provide the means of staying a fore-topmast from which the jib sails are set.

Shrouds – rigging of a sailing ship which give a mast its lateral support.

Belted Plaid – Feileadh Mor –Double width long cloth of woven tartan worn over the shoulder and fastened by a clasp. At the waist it was fastened by a belt making sure its lower length came to the knees.

Ceilidh – Evenings of story telling, drinking and dancing.

Halifax – Capital of Nova Scotia, Canada

Bannocks – Sort of Pancakes which can be toasted or baked; made out of oatmeal covered or mixed with a thin batter of eggs, milk and butter.

Byre – Barn for animals on a farm

Kirk – Church

Muir – Moorland

Braes – Hillsides

Skean or Sgian Dubh – Small knife worn in sock of highland dress – translated means black knife

Tommies – Nickname for British soldiers

Blighty – Military nickname for England

Arthur's seat – Extinct volcanic hill in the centre of Edinburgh

Jerry – Nickname given to German soldiers.

Shrapnel – Fragments of exploding shells